MICHAEL RHINEHEART, P.I.

THE LAST PRIVATE EYE

JOHN BIRKETT

AVON
PUBLISHERS OF BARD, CAMELOT, DISCUS AND FLARE BOOKS

THE LAST PRIVATE EYE is an original publication of Avon Books. This work has never before appeared in book form. This work is a novel. Any similarity to actual persons or events is purely coincidental.

AVON BOOKS
A division of
The Hearst Corporation
105 Madison Avenue
New York, New York 10016

Copyright © 1988 by John Birkett
Published by arrangement with the author
Library of Congress Catalog Card Number: 87-91682
ISBN: 0-380-75488-6

First Avon Books Printing: March 1988

AVON TRADEMARK REG. U.S. PAT. OFF. AND IN OTHER COUNTRIES, MARCA REGISTRADA, HECHO EN U.S.A.

Printed in the U.S.A.

K–R 10 9 8 7 6 5 4 3 2 1

This book is for Betty

And for Julie, Ellen, and Lynn

I'M A PRIVATE EYE...

"Is this some kind of joke?"

"No joke." He took out his wallet and showed her his license.

She studied it carefully. "Oh wow," she said finally, "you really *are* a private eye. Like Marlowe," she added.

"Who?"

"Philip Marlowe, the private eye."

Rhineheart kept a straight face. "Does he have an office here in town?"

Ms. Simpson laughed. "You know perfectly well he's a character in fiction."

"You a private eye fan?" Rhineheart asked.

She nodded eagerly.

"You know the part," Rhineheart said, "where the dick says, 'You mind if I come in and ask you a couple of questions?'?"

"Uh-huh."

"This is it."

ONE

It was opening day of the spring meet at Churchill Downs. A clear bright Saturday in late April. Rhineheart wasn't out at the track though. He was sitting in his office with his feet up on the desk, listening to the radio. Willie Nelson was singing about how the nightlife wasn't the good life.

When the telephone on his desk started to ring, he reached for it. Then, for some reason, he hesitated a moment, letting his hand hover over the receiver. It was just a second or two, a brief, meaningless gesture, but later, weeks later, when everything—the whole, sad, sorry mess that began that afternoon with that telephone call—was over, Rhineheart would remember that moment of hesitation.

He picked up the phone and a woman's voice—sonorous, somehow familiar—caught at his ear.

"I'd like to speak to Mr. Rhineheart, please."

"This is Rhineheart."

"Mickey?"

Rhineheart's first name was Michael. No one called him Mickey. Not anymore. Not since he was a kid anyway. Not since Saint Joseph's Elementary School on Market Street in the West End of Louisville. Even then, the nuns and all the other kids had called him Michael or just Rhineheart. Except for . . .

"Kate?" he said.

"Hi, Mickey."

1

Kate was Kathleen Sullivan. Red-haired. Pigtailed. Freckled. She had deep blue eyes and wore thick horn-rimmed glasses. She was Rhineheart's first girl friend. They had grown up together. Alphabetically, she had sat behind him in school from the second grade through the eighth. Rhineheart had not seen her since high school.

"Kate," he said. "It's been a long time."

"It's been almost twenty years, Mickey."

Twenty years. Twenty years ago Rhineheart had dropped out of high school and joined the army. He had heard, from someone, that Kate had gone on to college, had majored in broadcast journalism, and had gone to work as a reporter for a television station in Cincinnati.

"I heard you were up north," Rhineheart said.

"Not anymore," she said. "I've come back home. I've taken a job here. With Channel Six. I've been back almost a month."

Channel Six was a local TV station. An independent with a good reputation. It had won some awards for its regional news coverage.

"Are you married, Kate?"

"For the last ten years," she said. "I've got two kids, a boy and a girl. What about you, Mickey? Who's the lucky woman?"

Rhineheart had been married once. To a tall, slim woman with long brown hair and fine delicate features. Her name was Catherine. One afternoon, in the summer of 1976, she went for a ride on the expressway. A semi, traveling the opposite way, had jumped the divider. They had to use machinery to pull her body out of the tangle of metal. It had been a long time ago. Rhineheart never thought about it. Not when he could help it. He never talked about Catherine to anyone. Not ever.

"I'm not married," he said.

"I'm surprised. I thought you'd'd've been married three or four times by now. The way you used to go through women."

"I've been keeping myself for you, babe," Rhineheart said.

"Yeah, I'll bet."

"Tell me about yourself," Rhineheart said. "What have you been doing?"

Kate Sullivan told Rhineheart about the different stations she had worked for, in Cincinnati and Dayton and Cleveland, and the different jobs she had held, feature reporter, consumer correspondent, sports and weather person. She told Rhineheart about her husband, whose name was Jack, and who was in computers. She talked about her children, Megan, who was seven, and Kevin, the six-year-old. She'd come back to Louisville, she said, because Channel Six had made her an offer she couldn't refuse. She was going to be an investigative reporter, something she'd always wanted to do. The salary was great, and she had carte blanche to pursue whatever stories she wanted. And speaking of that . . . she wanted to see him.

"I may need your help in something," she said. "It's kind of important." Rhineheart caught a change in her tone, a new businesslike no-nonsense note in her voice. Her TV voice, he thought.

"What's the problem, babe?"

"Can we see each other?"

"Sure," Rhineheart said.

"When?"

"What about now?"

"Can we meet somewhere?"

He thought for a moment. "You know Baskerville's?" It was a restaurant—bar on South Third Street near the University of Louisville.

"Yes."

"Be in the bar," Rhineheart said. "I'll meet you there in half an hour."

The bar at Baskerville's was a dim cavernous room filled with high-backed armchairs and leather-covered booths. It was crowded, Rhineheart noted. A week from now, on Derby day, it would be empty. Everyone in town would be out at the Downs.

Kate Sullivan was seated in the corner. She stood up when she spotted Rhineheart and waved.

The freckles had disappeared, but the hair was as red as ever. A stylish shag, instead of pigtails, and the horn-rims were gone, replaced by oversized designer frames. Otherwise, she looked as if she hadn't gained a pound since the eighth grade. The same small-boned frame and bright, pretty face. She was wearing a beige blazer and a dark skirt and high heels and she looked very much, Rhineheart thought, like what they used to call a career woman.

She was a hugger and a kisser, Rhineheart remembered, as she got up on her tiptoes in order to plant one on his face and then wrapped her little arms around as much of him as she could.

"It's good to see you, babe."

She nodded, looking up at him. "You're as handsome as ever, Mickey."

Rhineheart said, "And you're a lot prettier than you were in the eighth grade."

She laughed. They sat down and a waitress materialized out of the gloom. Kate asked for a vodka-on-the-rocks, Rhineheart ordered Maker's Mark and water. The waitress smiled at him as if bourbon drinkers were her favorite kind of people and departed in the general direction of the bar.

"Now I want to know about you, Mickey," Kate said. "What have you been up to all these years?"

What had he been up to? Not very much, that was for sure. Certainly not the same things that everyone else had been up to—pursuing a career, raising a family. Catherine had been his only family, and after she died, his life had lost meaning and momentum. Everything suddenly seemed to require too much effort. He'd tried a couple of different occupations, then had more or less drifted into the investigation business. The years, it seemed, had gone by like a snap of the fingers. He'd somehow managed to survive. No small feat—but neither did it seem like any big deal.

Rhineheart shrugged. "I been staying busy," he said. The truth was that since Catherine the whole thing, except for a moment here and there, was a matter of just going through the motions. He stayed with it because what else was there? Most of the time he had trouble keeping his eyes open.

"You still shrug," Kate said with a smile. "It was always your favorite gesture. Whenever Sister Mary Hope would ask you what you were going to do with your life, you'd give her a shrug."

"Some things never change," Rhineheart said.

"You're a private detective now. What's that like?"

"It's a job," Rhineheart said. "It's all right."

"Do you like it?"

"It beats a lot of other jobs," Rhineheart said. "You don't have to sell anybody anything."

She laughed. "What's the best thing about it?"

Rhineheart shrugged. "The freedom. You're your own boss. You don't have to take a lot of . . . crap off people."

"You do what your clients ask of you, don't you?"

"If I feel like it."

"It must be nice to have that kind of independence."

"Yeah," Rhineheart said, "it is."

"Someone told me you were working for the government for a while."

Rhineheart nodded. "I used to be with the Commonwealth Attorney's office. As an investigator."

"That sounds kind of interesting."

"Yeah," he said. "It was, sort of. But I got fired. I couldn't handle the procedure."

"The procedure?"

"Following orders. Typing up reports. Stuff like that."

"Yes," she said, "you always had a tough time following orders."

The waitress returned with the drinks.

Rhineheart held up his glass for a toast. "Here's to the first girl I ever gave a valentine to."

"What a nice toast." Kate raised her glass to his. They clinked glasses and drank.

"Tell me about your work, Mickey. About some of the things you do."

"Such as?"

"Do you ever—" She hesitated. "Search for someone who's missing?"

"Sure," Rhineheart said. "I do divorce work too." He didn't add that he was broke right now and would do just about anything. If the money was right. And it was legal. And if he felt like doing it.

Kate reached into her purse and took out a snapshot and handed it to Rhineheart.

It was a color photograph of a blond-haired outdoorsy-looking guy. In his mid-thirties. Tall and thin, with a long, sharp face. He was wearing faded jeans and a T-shirt and was leaning on a whitewashed paddock fence. In the background were horse barns and rolling countryside.

"His name is Carl Walsh," she said. "He's been missing since Wednesday evening."

TWO

Rhineheart lit a cigarette. "This Walsh a friend?"

Kate Sullivan shook her head. "No. I taped an interview with him last spring when I was working for a Cincinnati station. A 'life on the racetrack' piece. Carl Walsh is a hot-walker, a stable hand. He works for Cresthill Farms. Are you familiar with Cresthill?"

Rhineheart nodded. Who wasn't familiar with Cresthill Farms? It was one of the largest horse farms in Kentucky, a big name in thoroughbred racing and breeding. Cresthill was owned by Duke and Jessica Kingston, two of the more colorful figures in Kentucky social circles. The Kingstons, who bred and raced their own horses, were rich and famous and flamboyant. They were renowned, among other things, for the big party they threw every year during Derby week. It was held in a tent on the grounds at Cresthill and was considered the social event of the racing season.

"Carl called me up this past Wednesday," she said. "He said he'd read in the paper that I was working in Louisville now, and he asked me if I remembered him from the interview. He said he had a story for me, one that would—his exact words were 'blow this town wide open.' I tried to get him to tell me more, but all he would say was that if certain things didn't work out he would tell me some news that involved the Derby and some very famous people."

Kate paused. She looked at Rhineheart as if she expected him to ask her something. When he didn't, she said, "You do know that Cresthill Farm has a horse in this year's Derby, don't you?"

Rhineheart nodded. Cresthill's Derby entry was a lightly raced and highly publicized three-year-old named Royal Dancer. The Kingstons had bought the horse a few years back at the Keeneland yearling sales and had paid a couple million for him. If Rhineheart remembered correctly, Royal Dancer had won a big stakes race in Florida earlier in the year, but had raced only once since then, lost, and was considered something of a long shot for the Derby.

"Did Walsh mention any names?" Rhineheart asked.

"No. He refused to say anything else. He gave me his phone number and his address and promised to call me the next day—Thursday. But he didn't. So I called him. His wife answered, her name is Rhonda. She said Carl had left the night before and hadn't come back. She seemed really upset. She promised to call me when Carl returned, but she didn't. I phoned her on Friday. There was no answer, Mickey. I went over to their apartment but no one was home. I talked to the manager of the apartment building, a girl named Karen Simpson. She said she hadn't seen Carl Walsh or his wife for a couple of days. Carl hasn't been to work either. I talked to his boss, the head trainer at Cresthill, an Englishman named John Hughes. He told me Carl was scheduled to come to work at six-thirty Thursday morning, but he never showed up. I hate to sound melodramatic, Mickey, but Carl Walsh seems to have... disappeared."

Rhineheart said, "And you want me to find him?"

Kate Sullivan nodded.

"Why me?" Rhineheart asked. "Why not some bigger agency? Some high-powered corporate security outfit with a lot of resources?"

Kate smiled. "I'm not old friends with any big-time security outfits."

"You didn't come to me because we went to grade school together, did you?"

"Don't worry," she said, "I asked around about you. You come highly recommended, Mickey. The station's legal counsel, Warren Fisher, said you were the best private investigator in Louisville."

Warren Fisher was an attorney Rhineheart had helped out of a jam once.

"He also said—and I'm quoting—that you were 'one tough dude.'"

Rhineheart took a sip of his drink.

"He also said—nicely, I might add—that you weren't entirely lacking in self-confidence."

Three for three, Rhineheart thought. Not bad for a lawyer.

"Will you try to find Carl Walsh for me, Mickey?"

Rhineheart thought about it. Cresthill Farms. Jet-set thoroughbred breeders. A Derby horse. It was a whole different league from the one he usually played in, but he didn't have any doubts he could handle it. And it sounded like the kind of case that wasn't likely to put him to sleep.

"I'll give it a shot," he said. "On one condition."

"What's that?"

"You stop calling me Mickey. It makes me feel like I'm back in the eighth grade and about to get my knuckles rapped by one of the nuns. Call me Mike, or Rhineheart, or anything. Except Mickey."

"I'm sorry, I didn't realize." She smiled at Rhineheart. "What about Michael? Is that okay?"

"Fine."

"Warren Fisher said to ask you about your fee."

"My fee," Rhineheart said, "is two hundred a day, plus expenses. Plus," he added, "I'll need a retainer. A thousand."

Kate didn't bat an eye. "No problem. The station is backing me fully in this. They've agreed to cover all your expenses. A check from the news department will be in the mail Monday morning."

"Good," Rhineheart said. "Now tell me why you haven't called the police in on this."

"I considered it," she said. "I gave it some serious thought. Then I decided not to. For one thing I'm not sure how efficient the police are in this kind of matter. For another, I can't rely on their keeping me informed. You see,

Michael, I want Carl Walsh found, but I also want an exclusive on whatever story there might be. You understand that?"

Rhineheart shrugged. "Sure." Kate was ambitious. She wanted to do a good job. There was nothing wrong with that.

She handed him a piece of paper that had MEMO FROM THE DESK OF KATHLEEN SULLIVAN written across the top. "Carl Walsh's address. My telephone numbers at home and at work. This"—she pointed to an entry—"is John Hughes's phone number and address."

"You got any strong feelings about where I ought to start on this?" Rhineheart asked. It was a standard question he put to all his clients.

"I wouldn't dream of suggesting how you go about your job, Michael. All I ask is that you keep me informed of your progress. I'd like daily reports, if that's possible."

"Sure," Rhineheart said. The truth was he made reports when he felt like it. Usually, as few as possible.

He asked Kate if she had a press pass for Churchill Downs.

"Yes."

He held out his hand. "Give it to me."

"But—"

"If I'm going to knock around and ask questions, I'll need access to the stable areas at the Downs."

"But won't they—"

"They never look at the names on them," Rhineheart said. "If you need a replacement, tell your station manager you lost yours."

She dug the pass out of her purse and handed it to Rhineheart. "You come on awfully strong, Michael. Are you as tough as you seem to be?"

Rhineheart smiled at her. "Tougher," he said. He finished off his drink, laid some bills on the table, stood up.

"It was good seeing you again," she said.

"Like old times," Rhineheart said. "Any last-minute instructions?"

"I can't think of any," she said. "And you'd probably just ignore them anyway."

She was right. "I'll be in touch, Kate," Rhineheart said, and walked out of the place.

THREE

On the way to Carl Walsh's apartment Rhineheart tried to recall what he knew or had heard about Duke Kingston. An ex-coal baron from eastern Kentucky, Kingston, the story went, had married money and in the course of a decade or so had become respectable. He had built Cresthill Farms into one of the finest racing stables in America. Cresthill horses had won most of the big stakes races in the country, but none had ever won the Derby. Kingston's desire to win the Kentucky Derby was legendary. There was nothing he wouldn't do, it was said, to see his colors in the winner's circle on the first Saturday in May.

Rhineheart didn't know if that were fact or racetrack rumor or what it had to do with a stable hand named Carl Walsh. Maybe in the course of things, he would find out.

Walsh lived in a squat redbrick apartment building that sat on a quiet, tree-lined street in the city's South End. Rhineheart parked his car—a beat-up '76 Maverick—out front, climbed the stairs to the second floor, and found Walsh's apartment at the end of a narrow, empty corridor.

He knocked on the door, waited, knocked again, waited a few minutes longer, then took out a credit card and went to work on the lock. Thirty seconds later, he stepped inside and closed the door behind him.

The place was a one-room studio apartment with a shag carpet, a bathroom off to the left, and a small kitchen area in the alcove near the front door.

An unmade double bed divided the room in two: sofa,

12

end tables, an armchair, and glass-topped coffee table on one side; night table, dresser, and a small walk-in closet on the other. A portable TV sat next to a phone on the night table.

Rhineheart gazed around the room. Nothing looked out of place. Not exactly. There were no obvious signs that the apartment had been searched, but he could tell that recently it had been taken apart and put back together. Systematically and methodically. By pros.

Operating on the notion that he might find something they had overlooked and on the principle that you had to begin somewhere, Rhineheart went into the bathroom and began looking through the medicine cabinet. He found a bottle of aspirin, a Gillette razor, a Lady Bic razor, a packet of throat lozenges, a can of Edge shaving cream, a tube of lipstick, a bottle of mouthwash, a box of Band-Aids, a tube of toothpaste, a thing of eye makeup, a plastic bag full of hair rollers, an empty shampoo bottle, a jar of Vaseline, a tube of lip ointment, and a small bottle of Absorbine Jr.

The bathroom hamper contained dirty towels.

The bathtub was dry. There was no soap in the soap dish.

He left the bathroom and walked back into the main room. Stacks of old *Daily Racing Forms* sat on the coffee table alongside back issues of *Cosmopolitan* and *Playboy* and *People*. He flipped through the *Forms* and the magazines, but found nothing significant, no clues or secret messages hidden between the pages.

Rhineheart ran his hands down the back and sides of the sofa and the chair: No loose change. Nothing.

Like a lot of investigative work, searching a place was a pain in the ass. Even if you knew what you were looking for. And he didn't.

On one of the end tables, he noticed a pack of matches lying there in plain sight for everyone to see. The purloined matchbook? He picked it up. The cover advertised the Red Wind Motel on Dixie Highway. Weekly Rates. On the inside of the cover someone had written *Room 24*.

Rhineheart stuck the matchbook in his pocket and walked over to the other side of the room. Hanging on the wall above the dresser were two framed color photographs. One was a shot of Walsh and a pretty frizzy-haired blonde. They were standing on the deck of a houseboat, their arms around each other, smiling at the camera. The words *Love, Rhonda* were scrawled in pen across the bottom of the photograph.

The other picture was one of those standard racetrack photographs: a shot of the winning horse, his owner, the owner's entourage, the trainer, the jockey, the horse's groom, and whatever stable help happened to be around.

The horse in the photograph was a rangy chestnut. There was no identification or date on the photo but Rhineheart was sure it was a shot of Royal Dancer taken after his stakes victory in Florida earlier in the year. There were eight to ten people standing posed in a semicircle around the horse. In the middle of the group stood Duke and Jessica Kingston, looking well dressed and rich and handsome. Rhineheart had heard she was a real beauty, but you couldn't tell a whole lot from the photo.

On the far left of the frame Carl Walsh stood looking solemnly at the camera.

Rhineheart went over to the dresser and began going through it drawer by drawer. The top drawer contained men's clothes, jeans, T-shirts, socks, underwear. The second and third drawers were full of women's stuff—sweaters, scarves, lingerie, all the same size. Walsh's wife had left her clothes behind. She must have left in a hurry.

The next two drawers were filled with letters and papers, gas bills and rent receipts, canceled checks and old pay stubs. Rhineheart rummaged around and came up with a pay stub dated March 12 from Saint Anthony's Hospital. It showed that Rhonda Walsh had cleared $213.23 that week.

The bottom drawer contained half a dozen programs from the recent Keeneland meeting and some uncashed mutuel tickets. On the back of one of the tickets was a telephone number written in ballpoint. It was a 548 number, which was a South End exchange. Rhineheart stuck the ticket in his pocket and wandered into the kitchen.

He opened drawers and cabinets, looked in the refrigerator. There were two full bags of garbage under the sink. He spread some newspaper out on the kitchen floor, dumped out the bags, and slowly and carefully went through the eggshells and empty milk cartons and food scraps. At the bottom of the pile he found something: a penciled list of words and initials on a stained and blotted sheet of lined paper.

It read:

DR. G   10:30 Wed.
Lewis WC
LANCELOT

Rhineheart smoothed out the sheet of paper, folded it, and stuck it in his pocket. He had no idea what any of it meant. He put the garbage back in the bags, washed his hands in the kitchen sink, then went into the main room, picked up the phone, and dialed the number of the Red Wind Motel.

The desk clerk answered.

Rhineheart asked the clerk to connect him to room 24.

"Just a minute, please." The phone rang half a dozen times. The clerk came back on the line. "I'm sorry, sir. Mr. Sanchez seems to be out. Can I take a message?"

"No thanks."

Next Rhineheart tried the 548 number. The phone rang twice, was picked up, and a man's nasal voice said, "Yeah?"

Rhineheart recognized the voice. It belonged to a small-time bookie he knew named Marvin Green. Marvin said, "C'mon, c'mon, what do you want, who is this?"

Rhineheart hung up and checked his watch. It was 4:15. He had been in the apartment a full hour. It was time to go. Rhineheart went into the bathroom, got a dirty towel, and wiped off everything he had touched. Then he walked over to the door and let himself out.

FOUR

Downstairs, on the first floor, the second door on the left had a brass plate that had MANAGER on it. The young woman who answered Rhineheart's knock had shoulder-length black hair, sexy eyes, good breasts, a slim waist, nice hips, and long shapely legs. She was wearing a red T-shirt, no bra, and skintight cutoffs. The trained investigator's eye for details, Rhineheart thought. Once again it had come in handy.

He wanted to talk to her about her body, tell her about her legs, say something about those fine hips, something on the order of "You've got a beautiful ass," but he was there on business. So he asked her if he could see the manager.

"Ah'm the manager." Her voice was soft, Southern. "My name is Karen Simpson."

"Mine's Rhineheart," he said. "I'm a private eye."

"A whut?" She did something with her eyelashes. They were thick and dark. Her eyes were large and violet-colored.

"A private detective."

Ms. Simpson looked amused. "This some kind of joke?"

"No joke." He took out his wallet and showed her his license.

She studied it carefully. "Oh, wow," she said finally, "you really *are* a private eye. Like Marlowe," she added. "Are you familiar with Marlowe?"

"Who?"

"Philip Marlowe, the private eye."

Philip Marlowe. Trouble is my business. Twenty-five dollars a day, plus expenses. For walking the mean streets of L.A." Rhineheart kept a straight face. "Does he have an office here in town?"

Ms. Simpson laughed. "You know perfectly well he doesn't have an office here. He's not real. He's a character in fiction. *The Big Sleep. Farewell, My Lovely.*"

"You a private-eye fan?" Rhineheart asked.

She nodded eagerly. "I was an English major in college. I did my senior term paper on the hard-boiled detective novel. I've probably read every private-eye novel ever written. Chandler. Hammett. Ross Macdonald. I've seen all the movies too."

She'd seen all the movies and read all the books.

"You know the part," Rhineheart said, "where the dick says, 'You mind if I come in and ask you a couple of questions?'?"

"Uh-huh."

"This is it."

She laughed and opened the door and showed him into a room that was a duplicate of Carl Walsh's apartment. Even the furniture looked the same. On the floor next to the bed was an exercise pad and some barbells.

"Excuse the mess," Ms. Simpson said. "You caught me in the middle of a workout."

"You lift weights?" Rhineheart asked.

"Just for muscle tone."

They look toned to me, Rhineheart barely stopped himself from saying. He took a seat in an overstuffed wing chair that turned out to be as uncomfortable as it looked. Ms. Simpson perched on the edge of the bed.

"Is this about the couple on the second floor?" she asked.

"How'd you guess?"

She shrugged. "First the reporter, then the police, now you."

"The police?"

She nodded. "This morning. Two of them. They searched Mr. Walsh's apartment."

"They ask you about Walsh?"

"Not really. All they seemed interested in doing was searching the place thoroughly. They were up there for *hours*."

"They leave with anything?"

"I don't think so, no, but I don't know for sure."

"What'd these police look like?"

"Two big guys. Wearing suits. One had a beard, the other was bald-headed." She paused and gave Rhineheart a look. "They weren't cops, were they?"

"I don't think so."

"Were they bad guys?"

"Probably."

"They looked like cops," she said.

"Don't worry about it," Rhineheart said. "Tell me about Walsh and his wife. What kind of people are they?"

"There's not much to tell. I don't know them very well. Hardly at all. I see them coming and going is about all. *He* left very suddenly a couple of days ago. I saw him come home around five o'clock Wednesday. He went upstairs for about an hour. Then he came downstairs, got in a cab, and left."

"A cab? What kind of a cab?"

"I don't remember."

"What color was it?"

She shrugged. "I'm sorry. I don't have a very good memory."

"What about his wife?"

"She works in a hospital. As a nurse's aide, I think."

"When was the last time you saw her?"

"Thursday."

"Did you see her leave?"

Ms. Simpson nodded. "She came downstairs around nine-thirty Thursday evening. She got into her car and drove off."

"What kind of car was she driving?"

"One of those Japanese cars. Yellow. I'm not good on makes. Or years."

Rhineheart stood up. "You've been very helpful, Ms. Simpson. I'll let you get back to your workout."

She smiled at him. "You could stay if you like." She

fluttered her lashes. "I've never balled a real private eye before," she said.

Rhineheart liked to think of himself as a fairly cool person who wasn't surprised by a whole hell of a lot. Still, there were times. It took him a moment to think up a reply. "We do it just like everyone else," he said.

"You know who you look like?" Ms. Simpson said. "The actor. Big, rough-looking guy. How tall are you, anyway?"

"What's height got to do with it?" he asked.

"Six two?"

Rhineheart nodded. "You're not going to ask me what I weigh, are you?"

Ms. Simpson shrugged. "I might." She stood and took off her T-shirt.

Rhineheart had been right. No bra.

"You want to do it on the floor or on the bed?"

It was one hell of a choice. "You don't want to get into anything with me," Rhineheart said. "I'm an old guy. Way over thirty."

"I've always had this passion for older men."

It was a great line. Rhinehcart couldn't remember what movie it had come from.

He gave it one last shot. "You sure about this?"

"Are you all *talk*," Ms. Simpson said, "or do you *do* anything?"

Rhineheart stood up and took off his sport coat. He began to unbutton his shirt. "I got an hour or so," he said, "then I got to be someplace."

FIVE

"How about I just ride along with you," McGraw said. "That way I'd be getting some practical experience, and you'd be getting some, ah, company."

"I don't want any company," Rhineheart said. He took a bite of cheeseburger, a sip of Coke. Rhineheart and McGraw were sitting in a back booth at O'Brien's Bar & Grill, a neighborhood bar in the East End. McGraw was drinking beer. It was seven-thirty according to the clock above the bar.

"You know what you are, Rhineheart?"

"Yeah," he said, "I know what I am. You know what you are, McGraw? A pain in the ass." Rhineheart looked around for Wanda Jean, the waitress. "You want another beer?" he asked McGraw.

"No," McGraw said. "I want to ride along with you. You promised me next time you got a case, you'd let me come along and help. You said you'd show me the ropes. You said you'd teach me how to become a private eye."

"You can't teach somebody to become a private eye," Rhineheart said. "Either they're a natural-born private eye or they're not. And you're not. For one thing, you're too small."

"Too small?" McGraw repeated angrily. "What the fuck are you talking about 'too small'? Where do you get off with that kind of shit?"

"How tall *are* you?" Rhineheart asked.

"I'm five feet one."

"Bullshit," he said. "You're four ten. Tops."

"Five one."

"Stand up."

McGraw stood up. Rhineheart was surprised. McGraw looked taller than usual. He glanced down at McGraw's feet and saw that she was wearing five-inch spike heels. They were red and they went with her black slacks and her white blouse. They were cute—like McGraw with her fried hair and her shapely little body. McGraw's first name was Sally. She was Rhineheart's secretary.

McGraw's big ambition in life was to become a private detective. She certainly had no future as a secretary, Rhineheart could swear to that. She typed twenty words a minute and misfiled every other piece of correspondence that came into the office. Rhineheart knew why he had hired her: she had bullshitted him into believing that she was a competent worker. What he couldn't figure out was why he kept her on. Pity, probably.

"Don't be looking at my shoes," McGraw said. "I'm five feet one, and besides, height's got nothing to do with it. You *promised*."

"I felt sorry for you," Rhineheart said. "You going to hold me to something I promised when I was feeling sorry for you?"

"Yeah," McGraw said, "I am."

"All that shit about being a woman and how tough it is and how nobody respects you."

"It's the truth, Rhineheart."

Wanda Jean came over to the booth. Wanda Jean had curly brown hair, a heart-shaped face, and a figure that overflowed whatever outfit she was wearing. She and Rhineheart were old friends.

To Rhineheart, Wanda Jean said, "You signal me, darlin'?"

"Give McGraw here another beer."

Wanda Jean said sure, but first she wanted to know how come Rhineheart never called her up anymore. Rhineheart said it was because he'd been busy. Wanda Jean said yeah, sure, she'd heard that shit before. She wanted to know when they were going to go out and hit some honky-tonk bars and do some serious drinking and dancing and who knew what else.

Rhineheart said that sounded good to him.

Wanda Jean winked at him and wandered off. Rhineheart looked over at McGraw, who was drumming her tiny fingers impatiently on the tabletop.

"You going to keep your promise to me, or not?"

"Where I'm going tonight," Rhineheart said, "it might be dangerous."

"That's fine with me," McGraw said.

"What do you mean, that's fine with you? Are you crazy?"

"Rhineheart, I'm sick of being just a secretary. Sitting around the office doing the same stuff day after day. It's boring and it's stupid."

"And you don't do it very well anyway," he added.

"Don't be a smart-ass," McGraw said. "It's not the kind of job anyone with any intelligence would do well. It's like being a housewife. It's a rotten job, Rhineheart. I want to do something different. Something exciting. I don't care if it's dangerous or not."

McGraw was like a lot of people, Rhineheart thought. She had the idea that private-eyeing was something special. The truth was that a lot of the time it was a matter of doing something like sitting around in your car outside a motel room, spying on some dude who was cheating on his wife.

"McGraw, being a private eye isn't that great a thing. It's mostly a lot of routine, boring shit."

"Yeah? If it's so bad, then how come you do it?"

"It's like I told Kate Sullivan," Rhineheart said. "It's one of the few jobs there is where you don't have to sell anybody anything."

"Yeah, well I don't like selling any better than you do, Rhineheart, and private-eyeing's a whole lot better than being a secretary."

Rhineheart gave her a long look. "I take you with me," he said, "you better be cool and do what I tell you."

McGraw, who was too small to lean across the booth, jumped to her feet, hustled over to the other side of the booth, grabbed hold of Rhineheart's face, and planted a loud wet kiss on his chin.

It was, he realized, the second time that day he had been kissed in a sisterly way by a little broad. When you stopped to think about it, McGraw had a lot of Kate Sullivan in her. Or vice versa. Maybe that was the reason he liked her.

"I promise to be cool," McGraw said. "I swear to do what you tell me." She sat back down and took a sip of beer. "Where we going first?"

Rhineheart shrugged.

Marvin Green hung around a place called the Kitty Kat Club, a topless joint on Cane Run Road. The Kitty Kat was owned by Angelo Corrati, who was wired, it was said, to one of the biggest families on the East Coast.

"You know who Angelo Corrati is?" he asked McGraw.

"The Mafia guy?"

"We're going to drop by his place of business, see what's going on."

The parking lot at the Kitty Kat Club was half-full. Rhineheart parked next to a tall neon sign that flashed WELCOME DERBY VISITORS in bright orange letters. On the way inside, McGraw said, "I've never been in here before."

"You'll love it," Rhineheart said, taking her by the elbow and steering her over to a corner table. The room was dimly lit, smoky. On a small stage near the bar a tired-looking nude dancer was doing her number to loud jukebox music.

McGraw, squinting across the room, plucked at Rhineheart's sleeve. "Rhineheart, that dancer is topless *and* bottomless."

"McGraw," Rhineheart said, "you are going to make one hell of a detective."

"Smart-ass."

A waitress in a kitten costume strolled up to the table. Rhineheart knew her. Her name, he remembered, was Barbara. Everyone called her Bobbie. It had been a few years since he had seen her. He wasn't sure she would recognize him.

"How you doing, Bobbie?"

"I'm doin' fine, Rhineheart. How you doin'?"

"I'm doing okay."

"I don't ever see you around anymore."

"I been kind of busy, babe."

McGraw said, "My name's Sally McGraw."

Bobbie ignored her. She said, "So what you been doin' with yourself, Rhineheart? You still a dicktective?"

"Yeah." He looked over at McGraw. "You want a beer?" McGraw nodded.

"Give McGraw here a beer," Rhineheart said, "and give me a Diet Coke, or something."

Bobbie looked surprised. "You want a *soft* drink?"

"I'm on the job, babe."

"Back in the old days, you didn't care if you were on the job, or not. You *always* drank bourbon."

"I'm getting old, Bobbie."

"Aren't we all," Bobbie said in a wistful little voice. Rhineheart watched her walk away toward the bar.

"Classy person," McGraw said.

"She's all right," Rhineheart said.

"You seem to know an awful lot of waitresses."

Rhineheart did his John Wayne imitation. "You think so, huh?"

When Bobbie returned with the drinks, Rhineheart asked her if Marvin Green had been in.

"Not tonight."

He showed her Carl Walsh's photograph. "You ever see this guy around here?"

Bobbie shook her head. "I don't think so."

Rhineheart asked her if Angelo Corrati still owned the place.

She nodded. "Uh-huh."

"He around?"

"He's in his office," she said, and slid her eyes toward a table near the door, where a thin, red-haired man in a checkered sport coat was sitting. "That's his table there. The redhead guy's waiting for him."

"Who's the guy?"

Bobbie shrugged. "Just some guy. He comes in." Bobbie started to walk away, then stopped and turned back. "I get off at two-thirty," she told Rhineheart, then turned again and bumped into a squat thick-necked man in a brown suit. She excused herself and walked away.

The man in the brown suit walked up to the table. He had thick, blunt features that seemed to be twisted into a permanent scowl. His voice was pure gravel.

"Rhineheart," he said.

"Katz."

"How's it going, peeper?"

"It's going okay."

Katz jerked his head at McGraw. "Who's the little lady?"

McGraw looked outraged. Before she could speak, Rhineheart said, "Katz, I want you meet Sally McGraw. Sally, this is Detective Sergeant Katz. Louisville poe-leece. Homicide."

Katz nodded at McGraw.

"McGraw's my—" Rhineheart began.

"I'm his associate," McGraw cut in.

Katz smirked. "A lady dick, eh?" He shook his head in obvious dismay. "What's the world coming to, Rhineheart?"

"You tell me, Katz."

"So what's going on?" Katz said. "You on a case, or what?"

Before Rhineheart could stop her, McGraw said, "We're looking for somebody named Carl Walsh."

Katz smiled. It didn't look a whole lot different from when he frowned. "Who's Carl Walsh, peeper?"

Rhineheart put some bills on the table and stood up. "I'll see you later, Katz." He took McGraw's arm and yanked her out of the booth.

"Come on, little lady. We're going to a motel."

SIX

The Red Wind Motel was on Dixie Highway, a few miles south of the Watterson Expressway. Two dozen whitewashed stucco cabins that curved around a parking lot shaped like an inverted U. Rhineheart pulled into the lot, parked, and checked his watch: 11:06 P.M. The night sky was black and moonless.

"Wait here," he told McGraw.

"Rhineheart," McGraw said, "I didn't come all the way out here to sit in the car and wait for you."

"All right," Rhineheart said. "But keep your mouth shut and do as I say, and if we see anyone, you better come on tough and act like you know what you're doing."

They got out of the car and walked across the lot. Room 24 was on the far end. A naked light bulb burned over the door. Rhineheart reached up and unscrewed the bulb. He knocked on the door. There was no response. When he put his ear against the door, he could hear the murmur of a television set from inside the room.

He took out his credit card and slipped it into the jamb.

"What are you doing?" McGraw asked in a loud whisper.

"This is what you call B and E, babe. It's a felony. Three to five, minimum."

"You mean we're doing something *illegal?*"

"Be quiet, goddammit."

Rhineheart opened the door. He pushed McGraw inside, stepped in after her, and closed the door. The room was dark except for the flickering glow of a black-and-white TV set against the far wall. He felt for the wall switch and flipped it on.

A small Hispanic man with a thin black mustache was lying on the bed. He was dressed the way racetrackers dress—faded jeans, a jean jacket, cowboy boots. His hands were folded across his stomach and he had a peaceful expression on his face. Rhineheart was pretty sure the man on the bed was named Sanchez. He would have asked him just to be sure, but the guy wasn't about to do any talking. He had a neat round bullet hole between his eyes. A thin line of dried blood ran down the side of his face.

McGraw stood in the center of the room, pointing at the body. Her face was pale, the hand that pointed trembled. "Is he . . . ? Is he . . . ?"

Rhineheart nodded. "Yeah." He walked over to the bed and touched his knuckles to the side of the man's face. The skin was cool, getting cold. "He's been dead for a while," Rhineheart said. "Ten or twelve hours."

McGraw nodded. She seemed unable to speak.

Rhineheart found himself staring past her at the TV set, where two actors dressed like farmers were trading one-liners. Their routine was punctuated by bursts of mechanical-sounding laughter. He walked over, switched off the set, and looked around the room. It wasn't much of a place to have died in. It never is, he thought.

The walls were peeling and the furniture—a chest of drawers, a table, and an armchair—looked cheap and squalid and plastic. There was a smell in the air, an acrid odor mixed with something sour and sleazy. It made Rhineheart's eyes blink and his nose run.

He looked over at McGraw, who was standing there, pale-faced, scared, waiting for him to tell her what to do. "Be cool," he told her. "Whatever we do here, whatever happens, we always stay cool. Hear?"

McGraw gulped, nodded.

"Go to the window," Rhineheart said.

McGraw walked to the window.

"Ease back the shade," Rhineheart said, "and check the outside."

McGraw did as she was told.

"What do you see out there?"

McGraw shook her head.

"Nothing?"

McGraw nodded.

"Say it," Rhineheart said.

"No-no one's out there."

"Good. Keep watching."

"Rhineheart?"

"Huh?"

"Wha-what do we do now?"

"We look around," he said. "We check things out."

"Do we call the police?"

Rhineheart gave her a look.

"Okay, okay. I'm sorry I asked."

Rhineheart searched the body first. He found some bills and loose change, a set of car keys, a pocket comb, and a wallet. The wallet contained a driver's license, a social security card, a photostatic copy of a naturalization certificate, and an employee's pass to Churchill Downs.

The pass was good for the current spring meet only, and was issued in the name of FELIX SANCHEZ, who was employed as an EXERCISE RIDER for RIVER CITY STUD.

River City Stud was a racing stable and breeding farm headquartered just outside Louisville in the eastern end of Jefferson County. It was owned by Howard Taggert, who sat on the board of directors at Churchill Downs, and was a prominent local horseman. Something tugged at Rhineheart's memory. In the back of his mind he knew something important about Taggert and River City, but for the life of him he couldn't remember what it was. It kept nagging at him while he searched the room.

Rhineheart went through it by the numbers, a crime-stopper's textbook search—slow, methodical, one end of the room to the other. He lifted the lid off the commode. He looked under the bed and behind the chest of drawers. It took him thirty-five minutes, and he didn't find a thing until he got to the closet. He was going through the clothes, item by item, when he felt something in the lining of a windbreaker.

It was a key that had slipped through a hole in the

pocket. The key had a green plastic tag that read LOCKER 741—STANDIFORD FIELD on it.

"What's that, Rhineheart?"

Rhineheart held it up.

"A key? Is it a clue?"

"A clue?" Rhineheart smiled. McGraw was something else. Maybe it *was* a clue.

"Rhineheart?"

He looked over at McGraw, who seemed less frightened, more relaxed.

"You want to know something?" McGraw said.

"Huh?"

"Earlier? I was scared there. For a minute."

"No kidding?" Rhineheart said. "I couldn't tell."

"Yes, you could, you lying son of a bitch." McGraw smiled. "But that's okay. I don't mind you bullshitting me once in a while."

Rhineheart stuck the key in his pocket and finished searching the closet. He took a towel from the bathroom and began wiping down the room.

"What are you doing now?"

"It's called erasing the evidence, babe. It's a felony, too."

There was some chance, he knew, that he was wiping away evidence left by the shooter. But only a small chance. The killing had all the earmarks of a professional job. It was doubtful that whoever did it had left any traces. At any rate, he didn't give a rat's ass about theoretical evidence that might or might not help the police. He wasn't having his or McGraw's fingerprints found in the room.

Ten minutes later he was finished. Throwing the towel in a corner, he walked over next to McGraw and looked out the window. Everything seemed cool. There were no people in the lot, no one around the cabins. On the way out the door, Rhineheart flipped off the light.

McGraw said, "I feel kind of bad about just leaving the guy lying in there."

"Me too," Rhineheart said, pulling the door shut.

They walked across the lot to the car and got in.

"Where we going now?" McGraw asked.

"*You're* going home," Rhineheart said. He started the

Maverick, shoved it into reverse, backed up, braked, shoved it into first, and wheeled out onto Dixie Highway, where he made an illegal U-turn and pointed the car toward the expressway.

He didn't say another word until they pulled up in front of McGraw's apartment building on the other side of town fifteen minutes later. Then he said, "You can keep working for me if you want to. You can do research. Legwork. You can run down information for me. Whatever you want to call it. But no more on-the-job training. Bringing you with me tonight was a bad move. Whatever this is I'm in, it's clear the people in it don't play. They waste people. I can't let you get involved in something this dangerous. You understand?"

McGraw was quiet; then after a minute, in a reluctant, grudging tone, she said, "I guess so."

"After a while," Rhineheart said, "after you learn the ropes, I'll take you down to the courthouse and you can apply for an investigator's license. I'll show you how to fill out the forms. Deal?"

"Deal."

"Then you can open your own office," he said. "Sally McGraw. Private eye."

McGraw managed a smile. "Sounds pretty good." She opened the door and got out. "Good night, Rhineheart."

"Good night, babe."

The airport locker area was in an aisleway around the corner from the Pan Am desk. Locker 741 was in the middle of a row of long, wide, double-sized lockers. Rhineheart stuck the key in the lock and twisted it open. A red-and-white Adidas traveling bag sat inside. He took it out, closed the locker, and walked over and sat down in one of the chairs near the window.

A clear plastic name tag was fixed to one of the handles: CARL WALSH. Rhineheart unzipped the bag. Inside was a syringe. A hypodermic syringe. Steel needle. Plastic plunger. It looked as if it had been used.

He zipped the bag up and sat there staring at the floor for a few minutes trying to figure out what the syringe meant. Then he got up and walked over to the pay phone against the wall. He dropped a quarter in the phone, punched out the emergency number, and in his best Bogart voice said, "Gimme the coppers, shweetheart. I wanna report a dead body."

SEVEN

The shrill ringing of the telephone woke Rhineheart up the next morning. He rolled over and picked up the receiver.

"Michael?" Kate Sullivan.

"Hello, Kate."

"Good morning, Michael. How are you?"

"I'm asleep," he said. "How about you?"

"I'm fine."

"Is there some reason you called?"

"Nothing special. I thought you might have learned something since our meeting yesterday. And naturally I want to be kept up to date."

"Naturally."

"Is something wrong, Michael?"

"What time is it?" he muttered.

"Eight-thirty."

"In the *morning?*"

"I just got back from mass," she said.

Mass? Jesus Christ. The last mass he had been to was in Latin. He looked over at the clock. It *was* eight-thirty. "Kate," he said, "there's something wrong with this connection. I'll call you back later." Rhineheart hung up and tried to go back to sleep, but the phone began to ring again almost immediately.

He snatched it up.

"Yeah?"

"I'd like to speak to Mr. Rhineheart, please."

A woman's voice. Well bred. Throaty. With a special kind of edge to it.

"This is Rhineheart."

"Mr. Rhineheart, my name is Jessica Kingston."

Rhineheart came awake. "Hello."

"How are you, Mr. Rhineheart?"

"Sleepy."

She laughed. "I take it you're not much of a morning person, Mr. Rhineheart."

"My heart doesn't start to beat until noon," Rhineheart said.

Jessica Kingston laughed again. "You'll have to forgive me for phoning you so early. But I called to ask you to come and see me this afternoon. I'll be in my box on the third floor of the clubhouse at Churchill Downs."

Jessica Kingston. Rhineheart had heard stories about her looks, her legendary beauty. The stories had men fighting over her in public, magazines offering her fabulous sums to appear on their covers, famous Hollywood producers trying to sign her to movie contracts.

"I'll see if I can make it," Rhineheart said. *See?* Who was he trying to kid?

"I hope you'll be able to, Mr. Rhineheart. I'm looking forward to meeting you. Good-bye."

Rhineheart got out of bed and began putting on his sweat clothes. When he was dressed he walked back over to the bed.

"Wanda Jean?"

Wanda Jean stirred, threw back a cover, blinked, sat up, yawned. "Huh?"

"You want to go jogging with me?"

Wanda Jean wrinkled her nose. "You kiddin', Rhineheart?"

Bellarmine College, a small Catholic liberal arts college whose buildings were scattered along a grassy hillside overlooking Newburg Road, was a five-minute drive from Rhineheart's apartment. On one end of the campus a quarter-mile cinder track circled a soccer field. Rhineheart parked the Maverick on the shoulder of the road, got out, did a few perfunctory stretching exercises, then ran five, slow, sweaty miles.

The track was crowded with people—runners, joggers, walkers, young people and old people, kids, mothers with babies, old guys in sweat pants, girls in shorts. Some of the women weren't exactly negligible. After a bit he found his running stride, and settled in behind a sandy-haired girl in yellow short shorts. She wore her hair in a long ponytail that bounced rhythmically against her lower back with each stride.

He was halfway through the fourth mile when he suddenly remembered what it was that was important about Howard Taggert and River City Stud. They had a horse in the Derby, also, a colt named . . . Calabrate. Calabrate had just come off a strong race in New York and was mentioned as a top contender for the Derby.

On the last lap he spotted McGraw seated under a shade tree at one end of the track. She was wearing jeans and a tank top and carrying a small straw purse. Rhineheart left the track and ran over to her.

She tossed him a towel. "You sweat a lot."

"It's a sign of high intelligence."

"Why were you following the girl in the yellow shorts?"

"I was practicing surveillance techniques," Rhineheart said.

"Sure."

They walked over to the Maverick. Rhineheart reached in the window and opened the glove compartment. He took out the syringe, and handed it to McGraw. "I want you to take this over to Frank Parker's lab and have him analyze it for me. I need to know what substances it contained. I already called Frank. He'll meet you there at two-thirty this afternoon." He handed McGraw a slip of paper. "Here's his address." Rhineheart slid behind the wheel and started the car.

McGraw stuck her head in the passenger's side window. "Where you going?"

"To see Jessica Kingston."

"No shit?"

"Private box. Third floor of the clubhouse. The whole bit."

"They say she's really something."

"I heard that."

"You better watch yourself, Rhineheart. The rich are . . . different from you and me."

"F. Scott Fitzgerald," Rhineheart said.

"That's right. You're not the only goddamn person around here who reads, you know."

"I need you to do something else," Rhineheart said. "Find out if Carl Walsh ever worked for River City Stud."

"Taggert's outfit?"

"Yeah."

"How do I do that?"

Rhineheart shrugged. "Call up the Thoroughbred Employment Agency. Tell them you're the new personnel director at Calumet Farms, and you're checking Walsh's job application. See if they have a file on him."

"Good idea."

"I'll call you later," Rhineheart said.

"Okay. And Rhineheart?"

"Huh?"

"Be careful."

Rhineheart drove home. Wanda Jean had left a note pinned to the pillow.

See U later
Love,
Wanda Jean

Rhineheart took a shower, shaved, and dressed in his best suit—a gray three-piece Cricketeer. He put on a tie. After all, he was going to call on Jessica Kingston.

As he left the apartment, his stomach was making hunger noises. He wanted a big breakfast—omelette, French toast, hot black coffee— served to him in a nice restaurant. He settled for a double cheeseburger, order of fries, and soft drink in a fast-food place on Bardstown Road.

While he ate, he read the Sunday paper, which was thick with news about the Derby and the week-long series of events—a steamboat race, a parade, various luncheons, dinners, and parties—that led up to the race.

One of the parties mentioned was, by the newspaper's

account, "the most famous soiree in America, the huge annual Derby gala hosted by the Master and Mistress of Cresthill Farms, Charles 'Duke' Kingston and his beautiful wife, Jessica."

According to the paper, "the big bash" was scheduled for Thursday evening and would be attended by the Duchess of Sussex and by a great many celebrities of movies and television and the media. The article went on to list the celebrities. Rhineheart recognized some of the names.

He turned to the sports section, which featured a long article entitled "The Derby Dozen," an obvious reference to the fact that, barring injuries and late withdrawals, twelve three-year-olds were going to run in the big race.

He skimmed through the article until he came to the parts that dealt with Calabrate and Royal Dancer.

On the basis of his rousing 2nd place finish in last week's Wood Memorial at Aqueduct, Calabrate, a local favorite, is considered one of the top half-dozen candidates to capture Saturday's Kentucky Derby.

Bred by Howard Taggert at River City Stud, the largest horse farm in Jefferson County, Calabrate seems to be rounding into top form for the Spring Classic.

His 2nd place finish in the Wood gives him 2 wins, 3 seconds, and a third in 6 starts since he opened his 3-year-old campaign in February with an impressive 3-length win in the Hooper Stakes at Hialeah.

His earnings of $234,978 places him third among those horses slated to start. Owner Taggert likes his colt's chances. "He's a nice kind of colt and he's got a first-rate chance to win the whole thing." Calabrate is trained by Eclipse-winning trainer Johnny Bowden and will be ridden on Saturday by his usual rider, Chris McLain.

Royal Dancer's seventh-place finish in last month's Arkansas Derby at the Hot Springs Oval still has trainer John Hughes shaking his head. "I don't have any excuse for him," said Hughes, the native of England who now trains for Cresthill Farms. "He just didn't run his race." Royal Dancer's owner, Charles "Duke" Kingston, the multimillionaire proprietor of Cresthill Farms, assured reporters that his colt would "run big" in Saturday's Classic. "We're winners at Cresthill and we think the Dancer has a shot at winning the whole thing."

However, most racing experts agree that the son of Royal Native has only a slim chance of capturing the eighth and featured race on Saturday's card. Currently listed at 7 to 1, Royal Dancer is expected to remain a long shot at post time.

Royal Dancer's rider in the Run for the Roses will be Julio Montez, whose mounts have won more than a $1,000,000 already this year. Montez, when queried about his colt's chances, was noncommittal. "Me and Dancer'll do the best we can."

Royal Dancer's final workout for the Derby is scheduled for Tuesday of this week.

Rhineheart felt a twinge of sympathy for Montez and for Royal Dancer. He had some idea what it was like to be a long shot. He had bet on enough of them. It looked as if he was working on one. As a private eye he was kind of a long shot himself. He worked alone. Out of a small office. He had no real connections. What were the odds on his finding Carl Walsh? 12 to 1? 20 to 1? Probably higher. Like Montez, he would do the best he could, too. Maybe it would be good enough.

EIGHT

The Kingstons' private box was located in Section G on the third floor of the Churchill Downs clubhouse. The box had six seats and was directly across from the winner's circle and midway between the sixteenth pole and the finish line. It adjoined the governer's box and offered a clear, unobstructed view of the track, its long stretch and wide, sweeping turns, the spacious grassy infield (which on Saturday would be jammed with 100,000 people), the backstretch on the other side of the infield, and beyond that, the backside stable area, rows of cinder-block stables with low-hanging green-painted roofs.

It was a nice seat all right, but Rhineheart wasn't looking at the view. He had his eyes on Jessica Kingston, who was seated across the box.

She was worth looking at. Tall, slim, and elegant, she was dressed in a red blazer and white linen slacks. She might have stepped out of an ad in the *New Yorker*. Her hair was light brown and she wore it pulled back from her face in a simple twist. She looked to be about Rhineheart's age—thirty-five or so. Her features—oval eyes, high cheekbones, aquiline nose—were firm and clear. She had dark gray eyes, and when she smiled at Rhineheart, his heart quickened and his throat got full. It had been a long time since anyone had had that kind of effect on him. He was going to have to be cool and watch himself.

The call to post for the upcoming race blared out over the public address system. A murmur swept through the crowded stands. Rhineheart looked down to the left and saw the horses begin to emerge from the paddock tunnel onto the track. They were picked up by riders on lead ponies and led single file up the track toward the quarter pole.

Jessica Kingston said, "Are you a gambling man, Mr. Rhineheart?" Her tone was pleasant, conversational. It was, Rhineheart thought, as if they were about to have a social chat. Well, maybe they were.

He nodded. "Once in a while, yeah."

"Do you have a pick in this race?"

Rhineheart shrugged. He'd looked the race over in the *Form*, but he hadn't been able to separate the horses. "Six horse doesn't look too bad," he said. "Who do *you* like?"

"I don't bet," Jessica Kingston said. "My husband's the gambler in the family." She was silent for a moment, then she said, "I suppose you're wondering why I asked you to come out here."

Rhineheart shook his head. "I don't spend a lot of time wondering about things. I figured you had a reason, wanted to talk to me about something. That's why I came."

She smiled. "You're very direct. I like that. I'll try to be direct, too. How's your investigation going? Have you found Carl Walsh yet?"

"How'd you know I was looking for Carl Walsh?"

"I have sources, Mr. Rhineheart. *And* a good deal of interest in the case. After all, Walsh works for us. For Cresthill."

A flash of brightly colored jockey's silks caught the corner of Rhineheart's eye. Down on the track the horses galloped past the finish line. They were headed for the clubhouse turn, then the backstretch, where they would begin their warm-up exercises.

"Is that why you asked me out here, Mrs. Kingston? To find out about the investigation?"

Jessica Kingston lit a cigarette with a slim gold lighter and blew out a thin stream of smoke. "No," she said, "I didn't ask you here to find out about the investigation. I want to talk to you about my husband."

Rhineheart glanced over at the infield tote board, which was flashing odds changes. The two horse was the 9 to 5 favorite. The horse he liked, the six, was a medium long shot at 7 to 1. At the bottom of the board the TIME OF DAY column read 1:53. The TIME REMAINING slot showed 6 minutes to post.

"You've never met him, have you?" Jessica Kingston asked.

"Never had the pleasure," Rhineheart said.

"Don't be so sure it's a pleasure, Mr. Rhineheart."

He looked over at her. Her gaze was direct, steady. "You trying to tell me something, Mrs. Kingston?"

"My husband wants to see you, Mr. Rhineheart. This afternoon, if that's possible. He wants you to come down to Cresthill. If it's convenient for you."

Convenient? Was she kidding? There was no way he'd pass up a visit to Cresthill Farms. Like most of the other big thoroughbred horse farms—Spendthrift, Calumet—it was located some seventy miles down the road, in Fayette County, outside of Lexington, in that area of Kentucky known as the Blue Grass.

"Sure," Rhineheart said. "What time?"

"Four o'clock?"

"Fine."

"I need to warn you about my husband, Mr. Rhineheart. He can be terribly intimidating."

"Well, I'm pretty good at not being intimidated, Mrs. Kingston."

"Yes, I'm sure you are, but there's more to it than that. My husband is a very powerful man. There are times when he can even be dangerous. Particularly in regard to his horses and the Derby. He's a man who's interested in one thing and one thing only: he wants to win the Kentucky Derby. He thinks he's going to this year with Royal Dancer. Perhaps he's right. At any rate, his hope of winning the Derby has become a kind of obsession. And in the process he's become a different person from the man I married. He's become ruthless, Mr. Rhineheart. There is nothing, and I mean *nothing,* he wouldn't do to win the Derby. If he thought, for example, that your investigation might get in the way of his plans, he might try to stop you."

"Why are you telling me all this, Mrs. Kingston?"

"It's no great secret that Duke and I do not get along very well. Our marriage has been a marriage in name only for several years now. For a number of reasons, most of them good, sound economic ones, we've never divorced, and probably never will. However, we are two very different people with different aims and interests, and there are times when our interests conflict. My interest lies in the farm itself and the breeding operation. We have a great tradition at Cresthill and my hope is to perpetuate and carry on the work of my father, Bull Parker, who wanted Cresthill Farms to be the greatest thoroughbred breeding farm in the world. I'm afraid that Duke's obsession, his fanatical desire to win the Derby, might lead him to do something that could bring everything crashing down around our heads."

Rhineheart squinted over at the backstretch. The horses were starting to warm up. If you were a private eye long enough, Rhineheart thought, you got to hear all the news and the gossip and the confessions. All the soap opera shit of the world.

"I'm being frank with you, Mr. Rhineheart, because I don't want anything bad to happen. I wanted to talk to you before Duke did. I wanted to warn you to be on your guard. Duke will do his best to intimidate you."

"I'll try to watch myself, Mrs. Kingston."

"Don't let him bully you, Mr. Rhineheart."

"I'll give it my best shot."

"At the same time you must try to avoid a confrontation with him."

"Don't worry, Mrs. Kingston."

"I think you'll do just fine," Jessica Kingston said. "You seem tough enough, and it's good that you have a sense of humor. You're going to need it when you meet my husband." She looked at her watch and stood up. "I have an appointment. I'm afraid I have to leave." She gave Rhineheart her hand. "Good luck on your investigation, Mr. Rhineheart. Perhaps we'll see each other again." She turned and left the box. He watched her walk up the aisle and through the exit. She was the kind of woman you watched until she was out of sight.

Rhineheart sat there for a few minutes thinking about

what she had said. Then he walked back to the betting
windows and bet $200 on the six horse to win.

He watched the race on a TV monitor in the grandstand.
It was a seven-furlong claiming race for three-year-olds
and up. The six, a barrel-chested dark brown gelding,
broke alertly, then dropped back and stayed just off the
leaders until the quarter pole when he began to make his
move. In the turn he passed three horses and was fighting
for the lead at the top of the stretch. But that was all he
had. Coming out of the turn he flattened out and his stride
began to shorten and horses began to pass him. He was on
the inside near the rail and stayed there, tired and lugging
in, all the way down the stretch. He finished eighth, beaten
twenty some lengths by the favorite, the two horse, who
won the race easily, going away.

Rhineheart threw away his ticket and walked over to the
clubhouse parking lot. He wheeled the Maverick out of the
lot and drove it around to the backside entrance on Longfield Avenue. He parked on the street and walked through
the gate. He showed Kate Sullivan's pass to the gate guard,
who barely glanced at it, and made his way over to Barn
24.

A young black kid with a bushy Afro and a T-shirt that
read CRESTHILL FARMS was mucking out one of the empty
stalls.

Rhineheart asked the kid if John Hughes was around.

"Ain't nobody around," the kid said. "Just me. And I
ain't nobody much."

"I know that feeling," Rhineheart told him.

"You look in the clubhouse bar?" the kid said. "Hughes
be anyplace, he be in the clubhouse bar."

Rhineheart offered the kid a cigarette.

"No thanks."

"You work for Cresthill long?" Rhineheart asked.

"Couple of years too long" was the reply.

"You know Carl Walsh?"

"Sure, I know Carl." The kid frowned at Rhineheart.
"Why? I mean, who's asking?"

Rhineheart showed him the license.

"Rhineheart, huh? You a private eye, huh?"

"Yeah."

"Like Magnum, huh?"

"Not quite."

"Get all the broads, drive around in them fast wheels, dress sharp."

"I got a '76 Maverick," Rhineheart said. "With a bad rear end. And my wardrobe's not that great either. This is my best suit."

"Magnum ask people questions, he gives them cash money."

Rhineheart took out a twenty.

"Shit, yeah," the kid said, "I know Carl. Carl is my old buddy. What you want to know about Carl, Magnum?"

"When was the last time you saw him?"

"Tuesday morning. Over by the track kitchen. He was talking to old whatshisface, the guy who owns River City Stud."

"Howard Taggert?"

"That's it."

"You didn't happen to overhear what they were talking about, did you?"

The kid shook his head.

"You ever met Walsh's wife?"

"Naw. I met a couple of his girl friends, but I never met his old lady."

"Tell me about his girl friends."

"What's to tell, man. Waitress-type broads."

"You know any of them?"

"That twenty you holdin' keeps looking smaller and smaller."

"I got a twin to go with it if you keep on talking and tell me what I want to hear."

"Tammy somethin'. Irish last name. The Hideaway Bar and Grill. Over on Seventh Street Road. Little bitty broad. Too young for me."

"Carl likes the young ones, huh?"

"Shit, Carl likes 'em young and old and in between. And every other fucking way, too. Carl is a wild dude, man."

"Carl gamble?"

The kid cracked up. "Does a bear shit in the woods?"

"Who's he gamble with?"

"Anybody that'll take his money. Mostly with a dude named Marvin."

"I know Marvin," Rhineheart said.

"Everybody knows Marvin."

"You got any idea where Carl might be?"

"Be?" The kid looked puzzled. "Is he gone somewhere?"

"He hasn't been to work since Thursday, has he?"

"I don't know. I don't keep track of the dude's hours, man. Now that you mention it, I guess he ain't been around in a couple of days."

"You know any reason why he'd blow his job and disappear?"

"Maybe he just went out and got drunk and is sleeping it off somewhere."

"Three days is a pretty long sleeping it off."

The kid shrugged. "Carl a pretty wild dude, man. He be capable of a whole lot of shit."

"What about around here? Anything happen to him that might make him want to leave?"

"John Hughes jumped all *over* his shit last week, but that ain't nothin' new. He jumps in everybody's shit regular."

"What'd he get on Walsh for?"

"I don't know, but it was a bad scene. Lots of shoutin' and shit out behind the barn. They almost came to blows." The kid looked around. "Hughes come back and find me bullshittin' with you, and he's gonna jump in *my* shit. This ain't the best job in the world, but it's the only one I got. You know what I mean?"

Rhineheart gave him the first twenty, plus another one. "Thanks, kid, you been a big help."

"Anytime, Magnum."

Rhineheart started to walk away.

"Hey, Magnum."

Rhineheart stopped and turned around.

"Shea. That's her name. Tammy Shea."

NINE

Rhineheart pointed the Maverick east out of Louisville on I-64. A sign on the side of the road read LEXINGTON 73. Open countryside rolled away from the highway on both sides. Fields. Farmlands. Woods. Clumps of tall, dark green cedar trees dotted the side of the road. The only buildings he saw for long stretches were farm structures— sheds, tobacco barns, silos, farmhouses. The sun, straight overhead, beat down on the Maverick as it rolled past signs announcing approaches to different small towns—SHELBY-VILLE, WADDY-PEYTONA, LAWRENCEBURG.

He passed through Shelby and Franklin counties and turned off I-64 onto KY 60. He was in Woodford County now, the beginnings of thoroughbred country. He cruised through Midway, a drowsy little place in the road, and turned left on the Versailles Road. Just inside the Fayette County line he turned left again onto one of the side roads that led off the main highway. A few miles down the road he pulled over and came to a stop in front of the main entrance to Cresthill Farms.

The entrance was flanked by stone pillars six feet tall, bearing the Kingston name. Through the wrought-iron gate, across a stretch of ground the size of a city park, Rhineheart could see a redbrick Georgian-style mansion with tall, slim, white columns that formed a portico. It sat atop a small hill above a grove of ash trees. There might have been better words to describe it, but *stately* was the word that came to him.

Rhineheart got out of the car and rang the bell that was set into the side of one of the pillars. After a moment the gates swung open. He got back in the Maverick and drove in, onto a blacktop road that was lined with pink and white dogwood and magnolia trees. Off to the right, on the other side of a running creek, stood a cluster of horse barns and farm buildings. The barns and buildings were frame or clapboard and were painted royal blue and green, the Kingston racing colors. On each side of the blacktop, white oak-plank fences stretched off into the distance. On a sweep of lawn near the mansion a group of workers was putting up what looked like huge tent poles.

The road twisted through a corridor of ash trees and burr oaks and ended in a cemented parking area at the rear of the mansion. Rhineheart eased the Maverick into a spot between a black Mercedes and a steel gray Rolls Royce Silver Spirit.

He got out of the car and stood there for a moment, looking up at the house. It was a hell of a place. The old plantation. It made him feel like a sleazy private eye. A guy who made a couple of hundred a day when he worked and drove a twelve-year-old Maverick with a bad clutch. Someone who lived in a furnished apartment. Someone who drank too much and slept with a lot of waitresses.

What the hell, Rhineheart thought, that's what I am.

He walked around to the front door and rang the bell. A thin, sour-faced black woman answered the door.

"Yes?"

"You one of the slaves?" Rhineheart said.

"I beg your pardon?"

"Honky humor," Rhineheart said. "Pay no attention. The name's Rhineheart. I've got an appointment with Mr. Kingston."

"Come in, please."

In the entrance hall, Rhineheart tried to be cool and not gawk at the crystal chandelier, the winding staircase, and the gilt-edged mirror that took up most of one wall.

"This way, please."

He followed the maid down a short hallway, through a couple of tastefully furnished rooms, into a longer hallway where she stopped in front of a massive mahogany door.

"Mr. Kingston's library," she said, knocked, and departed back down the hallway.

"Come in," a voice said.

Rhineheart opened the door and more or less sauntered into the room. John Wayne, he thought, strolling into the Last Chance Saloon. It was a spacious, high-ceilinged room lined with books on three sides. A long conference table that looked like it belonged in some corporation boardroom stood in front of the fireplace. The fourth wall was a wide pair of French doors that looked out on an elaborate garden with trellised arbors and stone sculpture.

There were two people in the room. One was an enormous goon in a business suit who stood near the windows, as if he were guarding them. He had meat hooks for hands and a mean half-witted look on his otherwise blank face. The other one, the rich-looking bastard sitting behind the polished mahogany desk, Rhineheart was sure, was Duke Kingston.

Kingston had a crop of thick, silver hair, dark eyebrows, clear cold gray eyes, and a lean handsome face. He was trim and tanned and looked about as sophisticated and wealthy and aristocratic as it was possible to look. He stood up and came around the desk with his hand out.

"Duke Kingston." The accent, Rhineheart noted, was Deep South, a plantation owner's drawl.

"Michael Rhineheart."

"Supah. Supah," Kingston said, as they shook hands. "Pleasure to meet you, Mr. Rhineheart." Kingston jerked a thumb at the goon. "This here's Mr. Borchek."

Borchek nodded like someone who had been trained to nod.

"Mr. Borchek's one of my security consultants," Kingston said.

Bodyguard, Rhineheart thought. Arm breaker.

"What kind of name is Rhineheart?" Kingston seemed genuinely interested. "German?"

"Yeah."

"I'm a great admirer of the Germans," Kingston said. "Very industrious group of people, don't you think?"

Rhineheart made no reply. He wasn't about to get sucked into any yessir-nosir dialogue.

"There's people," Duke Kingston said, "not unintelligent people, who say we should've got together with them during World War II and went after the Communists." Kingston pronounced it *Common-ists*.

"You ask me here to talk about history?" Rhineheart said.

Kingston looked surprised, but managed a laugh.

"Mistah, you got a sense of humor."

"That's what your wife said. She seemed to think I'd need one."

"She did, huh? Well, that sounds like Jessica, all right." Kingston indicated a leather wing chair. "Have a seat, Mr. Rhineheart."

Rhineheart sat down and looked around the room. "Your wife not going to join us?"

Kingston shook his head. "You look disappointed, Mr. Rhineheart."

"I am."

"Too bad. Jessica is off somewhere, as usual, attending to something or other, some social function or civic meeting. It's in the nature of women to occupy themselves with such things. Frankly, I'm glad she's not here. We have some weighty matters to discuss, and I always find that when you're talking about something truly important, women just tend to get in the way. How you feel about that, Mr. Rhineheart?"

"I don't agree," Rhineheart said.

"No?" Duke Kingston raised an eyebrow. "Well, I got to admit that comes as something of a surprise to me. You don't look like the kind of man who takes much shit from women."

"I don't take shit from anybody," Rhineheart said.

"Not even a little bit, huh? Well, that's good to hear, Rhineheart. That's the kind of man I would like to have working for me. Someone who doesn't take any shit. I'm tired"—*tired* came out *tard*— "of all these ass kissers and brown nosers I'm surrounded by. I think you and me going to get along just supah." He walked back behind the desk, sat down, reached over and flipped open an elaborately carved cigar box. "Have a cigar, Mr. Rhineheart."

"No thanks."

"Go ahead," Duke Kingston urged. "They Cuban. Got a friend in the Diplomatic Corps keeps me supplied."

"Thanks, but no thanks."

Duke Kingston showed Rhineheart a mouthful of even, white teeth. "You a very polite young man. That's good to see. You don't meet folks with a lot of manners anymore."

"Actually," Rhineheart said, "my manners aren't all that great."

Kingston nodded. "Well, to tell you the truth, Mr. Rhineheart, neither are mine. Don't let this place and all these trappings fool you. Behind these expensive clothes, I'm just a rough ol' countryboy with simple tastes. I like simple things and plain talk."

Why don't you stop bullshitting around then, Rhineheart thought, and get to the point. "What exactly did you want to see me about?" he asked.

"Well," Kingston said, "for one thing, I'd like to know how your investigation's proceeding."

"What investigation is that?"

Kingston flashed more teeth. "Mr. Rhineheart, I keep abreast of things. Particularly when they involve either me or projects I'm interested in. I know you're looking for one of my employees, Carl Walsh. I know that Kathleen Sullivan hired you. I even know what she's paying you."

"You're pretty well informed, huh?"

Kingston nodded.

"Yeah, you could put it like that. The truth is, I'm a majority stockholder in that television station Miss Sullivan works for. Now, I'm not crude enough to suggest that I'm the one paying your salary, but you might could say I have more than a little interest in the matter. Particularly, when you consider that Carl Walsh works for me."

Rhineheart decided to play along a little. It was possible he might learn something from Kingston. "What is it you want to know?" Rhineheart asked.

"You got any leads yet on where Walsh might be?"

Rhineheart shrugged. "Not really."

"What's that mean?"

"It means I haven't got any *leads* as you call them. I've

just started my investigation," he said. "I need to look around, check out some things."

"What sort of things?"

"Things," Rhineheart said. "Nothing worth talking about. Yet."

Kingston sniffled. "You not very responsive," he said. "What's the problem? The station not paying you enough money?" Kingston grimaced, as if the thought of anyone making as little as Rhineheart was too much to bear. "I admit two hundred and fifty a day ain't much. It doesn't take me that long"—he snapped his fingers—"to make two fifty, but still and all, it seems like a lot to pay someone and get no real results."

He wagged a finger at Rhineheart. "You going to have to do better, Mr. Rhineheart, if you want to keep your job. Take it from me, I know this Sullivan woman's reputation and she won't tolerate no half-ass performance. She wants results, and she's a tough woman to please."

The man, Rhineheart thought, is trying to make me angry. "The way I figure it," he said pleasantly, "if Ms. Sullivan's not satisfied, she can always fire me."

Kingston looked glum. He rose from his chair and walked over to a sideboard that held whiskey bottles, decanters, glasses. His back turned, he began to mix a drink. "You like bourbon, Mr. Rhineheart?"

"Love it," Rhineheart said.

"I thought you looked like a drinking man," Kingston said. "As a matter of fact, someone told me you liked to drink a little." He turned and held up a bottle. "Eight-year-old hundred-proof bottled in bond suit you?"

"I'll pass," Rhineheart said.

"You sure?"

"Positive."

"What's the matter, Mr. Rhineheart? I thought you said you were a bourbon man."

"I gave it up for Lent," Rhineheart said.

Kingston snickered. "I believe you having me on, Mr. Rhineheart. But that's all right. What's life without a little joke, huh?" He returned to the desk with a tall glass in his hand. "You don't mind me having one, do you?"

"Knock yourself out," Rhineheart said. He jerked a thumb at the goon. "Maybe Mr. Borchek would like one."

"Mr. Borchek doesn't drink. At any rate, he's on duty." Kingston sipped his drink, set the glass down on the desk, and cleared his throat. "Let's get down to cases, Mr. Rhineheart. One of my stable hands is missing, disappeared into thin air, and this TV lady decides to hire a private detective to find him. That's fine, but all this occurs in the midst of the most important week of the year. It's only six days to the Derby. You got any conception what winning the Kentucky Derby means to a horseman, mistah?"

Rhineheart nodded. It was, he knew, the stuff that dreams were made of.

"I'm going to be brutally honest with you, Mr. Rhineheart. The Derby means more to me than just about anything. My lifelong ambition is to win it. I'd do just about anything to accomplish that goal. Maybe Jessica's already told you that. There's people say I'm something of a fanatic when it comes to the Derby. They may be right. I've entered horses in it that didn't have a prayer or a blind hope. All 'cause I wanted to win it so bad. Now, for the first time in years, I think I got a decent shot at it with Royal Dancer. I know the so-called experts don't think much of his chances, but he's the best horse I ever owned, a genuine stakes winner, and I want him to have his chance. I don't want any kind of disruption. That's why I'm prepared to double whatever salary this woman's paying you and offer you an additional ten-thousand-dollar bonus if you can find Carl Walsh before Thursday."

"Why Thursday?" Rhineheart asked.

"Thursday," Kingston said, "is the day they draw for post for the race. It's also the day of Jessica's big Derby party. I want everything smooth from then on out."

Rhineheart wanted to get it straight. "You asked me out here to offer me this?"

Kingston nodded. "Ten thousand dollars is a hell of a lot of money."

Rhineheart nodded. "Yeah," he said, "it is, isn't it."

Kingston smiled. "I thought you might think so." He

took a cigar out of the box and rolled it between his fingers. "And here's the thing, Mr. Rhineheart . . . I don't see any need to inform Mizz Sullivan about this. Or Jessica. It can be a little arrangement between us. A confidential matter." He paused. "What do you say?"

It was, Rhineheart knew, way too early in the game to be laying down any cards. "I'll give it some thought," he said.

"Fair enough," Kingston said. He stood up. "Get back to me on this, Mr. Rhineheart, and we'll work something out." He gestured to Borchek, who walked over and opened the door and stood there holding it open.

It looked as if the interview or meeting or whatever the hell it had been was over. Rhineheart stood up and walked over to the door. He had to look up to meet Borchek's eye. The goon was three inches taller and thirty pounds heavier, and standing next to him, Rhineheart could feel the man's brutality emanating from the man, like body odor.

"Tell me something," Rhineheart spoke to Kingston.

Kingston waved the cigar expansively. "Anythin'."

"What do *you* think happened to Carl Walsh?"

"I got no idea, Mr. Rhineheart."

"You think Howard Taggert might know?"

Kingston looked surprised. "Howard Taggert?"

"You know who Howard Taggert is, don't you?"

"Sho. As a matter of fact, Howard and I are old friends."

"You happen to know if Carl Walsh ever worked for him?"

Kingston shook his head. "Why don't you go and see Howard and ask him your ownself?"

"I might just do that," Rhineheart said. He started to leave, then stopped. "One more thing."

"What's that?"

"You don't mind if I talk to your stable help, do you?"

"Not at all," Kingston said. "Talk to anyone you please, Mr. Rhineheart."

Rhineheart stepped out into the hallway. The library door swung shut. The maid appeared at the end of the hallway and as he followed her back through the house,

Rhineheart remembered the photograph of the Kingstons he had seen on Walsh's wall. They said pictures never lied, but he couldn't see much resemblance between the handsome smiling couple in the photo and the two people he had met this afternoon.

TEN

On the drive back to Louisville Rhineheart thought about the case, trying to form some picture of it in his mind. What it reminded him of was the design of a crazy quilt he had once seen, a mixture of elements and ingredients that didn't seem to fit, yet appeared to be somehow related.

The disappearance of a stable hand and his wife. A dead man in a motel room. A story that would "blow the town wide open." Duke and Jessica Kingston. Howard Taggert. A pair of Derby horses. A bookie's telephone number. A locker key. A syringe. What the hell did it all mean?

Rhineheart didn't know. He was the first to admit that he wasn't hitting on much when it came to solving puzzles. His talent was for hanging in there, plodding along, poking around, and uncovering things. It occurred to him that he was going to need some help on this one. Farnsworth, Rhineheart thought. If there was anyone who could help him find the answers in this case, it was old Farnsworth. Everything Rhineheart knew about detecting had been taught to him by Farnsworth.

Tomorrow, Rhineheart decided, he would go and see the old pro, talk to him about the case, hear what Farnsworth had to say. Just thinking about bringing the old man in on it improved Rhineheart's mood. He switched on the radio and found an FM station that featured old-timey jazz. He drove back to Louisville with the tinny sounds of a 1920 New Orleans jazz band beating against his ears.

It was after five when he got back. He stopped at a gas station near the expressway and telephoned Cresthill's head trainer, John Hughes, but there was no answer.

He ate dinner at a Chinese restaurant in Jeffersontown. Moo Goo Gai Pan, fried rice, and hot tea. Dessert was a scoop of ice cream and a fortune cookie. The paper in the cookie read, *The star of riches will soon shine upon you*.

He called McGraw at home. The news on the syringe was negative. Frank Parker couldn't identify whatever substances were in the syringe. He was going to have to run more tests. He wanted Rhineheart to call him.

"You find out anything about Walsh?" Rhineheart asked McGraw.

"You bet your ass I did," McGraw said. "You were right. Walsh worked for River City Stud for two years. He left there to go to Cresthill. I got all this from a clerk at Thoroughbred Employment. It's on Walsh's job application."

"Good work," Rhineheart said. "You going to be at O'Brien's later?"

"I wasn't planning on it, no."

"I just got back from Cresthill Farms. I'll buy you a beer and tell you about it."

"I'll see you there about nine."

The Hideaway Club was a long, narrow shotgun of a room with a bar on one wall, a row of booths on the other, and a dozen tables in between. The decor was early redneck. Rhineheart slid into one of the empty booths and looked around. Even though it was Sunday the place was packed and noisy. All the tables were taken and the bar was crowded with loud, rowdy cowboy types in jeans and Western hats.

The jukebox was playing a Merle Haggard number. On the wall above the bar, a poster advertised a C&W radio station that played "Lovin', Lyin', Laughin', Cryin', Cheatin', Hurtin', Flirtin'" music.

A slim dark-haired girl with a sweet innocent face approached the booth. She was carrying a tray and holding a bar rag in one hand. She was wearing a denim mini skirt and white knee-high boots.

"Get you somethin'?"

Rhineheart took a gamble. "Hello, Tammy."

She smiled at him. "Do I know you?"

"I think so, yeah."

"I don't believe I know you."

"I'm a friend of Carl's."

The smile vanished. Her voice turned cold and unfriendly. "What do you want?"

"I'd like to talk to you for a minute."

She shook her head. "I got no time to talk. I'm busy."

"I'm trying to get in touch with Carl."

She laughed, a hollow little laugh. "Join the club, mister. Looks like ever'body's trying to get in touch with Carl. Only Carl ain't here. Carl took off. And *nobody* knows where he is. Not his good-for-nothin' buddies. Not his sweet little thang of a wife. Not even me. His girl friend. His *ex*–girl friend. The dumb-ass who believed all his lies and his bullshit, and believe me, mister, it was *all* bullshit."

"You got any idea where Carl might be?"

She smiled bitterly. "Ask his wife—if you can find her. I hear she's split too. It wouldn't surprise me none if they're together someplace. Look," she said, "it's like I told them other two guys, I don't give a royal shit where Carl Walsh is. He could be dead and it wouldn't make me no matter. And if you find him you can tell him I said that."

"Tell me about these two guys," Rhineheart said. "They were looking for Carl?"

Tammy nodded grudgingly. "They said they were cops, but they weren't. I can tell cops."

"One bald-headed, the other with a beard?"

Tammy nodded. "They offered me money if I'd tell them where Carl was. They acted like they didn't believe me when I said I didn't know."

"When was the last time you saw Carl?"

She shrugged. "I don't know. Tuesday, I guess. He

was supposed to call me Wednesday night, but he never did. The low-life son of a bitch." She swiped at the table with her bar rag. "Who are you, anyway—some kind of cop?"

Rhineheart said, "I'm a private investigator."

"A private investigator? You mean like on TV?"

"Not exactly."

"What are you looking for Carl for?"

"Someone hired me."

"His wife? Are you working for that bitch?"

"No."

"Then *who?*"

"I can't tell you that," Rhineheart said. He took a card out of his pocket and handed it to her.

"What's this?" She peered down at it.

"That's my address and phone number. I'd like you to call me if Carl gets in touch with you."

Tammy made a sound with her lips. "Fat chance."

"What makes you so sure that Carl left town?"

She frowned at Rhineheart. "What do you mean?"

"Maybe something happened to him," he said. "Maybe he got in some kind of accident. Maybe he couldn't get to a phone."

Tammy turned pale. "What are you talking about?" she said. "You don't know what you're talking about." She began to back away from the table. "I don't want to talk to you anymore. You come in here with all these questions and all this shit."

She threw the card on the floor and started to turn away.

Rhineheart stood up and caught hold of her arm. "Tammy, wait a minute—"

"Let go of me, you son of a bitch," she said in a loud voice. He dropped her arm and watched her stalk off across the room.

The place, Rhineheart noticed, was awfully and suddenly silent. The song on the jukebox had ended. He looked around to see a dozen rednecks and good old boys directing bad looks his way. Oh shit. Time to decamp. Rhineheart turned and strolled, cool and easy, toward the exit.

At the door, the bouncer, a thick-necked biker type with

a bushy beard and a black bandanna wrapped around his forehead, stepped in front of him.

"Where you going, chump?"

Rhineheart sized the bouncer up. The dude was a cruncher. He was probably going to have to use something. Like a chair. Or a table. Or a tank.

Politely, Rhineheart said, "Step out of my way, asshole."

"You were messing with Tammy, man. You put your hands on her, motherfucker."

"I'll tell you once more," Rhineheart said. "Get out of my way."

"Whip his ass, Moose," someone shouted from one of the tables.

Rhineheart turned to see where the voice was coming from, then turned back to find a roundhouse right coming his way. He stepped inside the swing and threw a quick left jab—right cross to the guy's face.

It was a pretty-looking combination, executed with style and grace. The trouble was the blows didn't seem to have a whole lot of effect on his opponent, who didn't even stagger, just reared back and started throwing roundhouse rights at Rhineheart's head.

Rhineheart backpedaled a few steps, jabbed the bouncer's face a couple of times. Blood began to dribble from the guy's nose. Rhineheart feinted with his left, then threw a short hard uppercut that made the guy grunt and rock back on his heels. Hitting the dude was something like hitting a tree trunk. Rhineheart was circling to his left when one of the bouncer's punches caught him on the shoulder. It knocked Rhineheart three feet sideways. His left side went numb.

Fuck this, Rhineheart thought. He reached over and picked up someone's beer off a table. He cracked the bottle over the bouncer's skull. The guy's knees buckled and he dropped to the floor like a sack of flour. Rhineheart kicked him once in the side to keep him down. Then he turned around and faced the room.

"Who's next?" he said. No one moved. No one said anything. He turned and left the place. As he crossed the lot to his car he started to whistle "West End Blues." Rhineheart's version of the tune was based on the 1929 recording by Louis Armstrong's Hot Five, with Jimmy Strong on clarinet and Earl "Fatha" Hines on the piano.

ELEVEN

Twenty minutes later Rhineheart was in O'Brien's sitting across the booth from McGraw.

"What was Jessica Kingston like?" McGraw wanted to know.

"She was all right," Rhineheart said.

"You like her?"

"She's not bad."

"You liked her. I can tell. You were impressed. Is she as beautiful as they say?"

"Yeah."

"So how did it go at Cresthill?"

"Just supah," Rhineheart said. "They're thinking about making me private eye to the rich and famous. Pretty soon I'll be able to open up branch offices in the suburbs. Shopping centers. Shit like that."

"What's Duke Kingston like?"

"He's different," Rhineheart said.

"Is he an asshole?"

He shrugged, looking around the room for Wanda Jean.

"She's off tonight," McGraw said. "Wanna go to a movie?"

"I don't think so," Rhineheart said.

"What are you going to do? Just sit here and get sloshed and think about Jessica Kingston?"

"I might."

"The Maltese Falcon," McGraw said.

The Maltese Falcon? Warner Brothers, 1941. Written and directed by John Huston. From the novel by Dashiell Hammett. Bogart. Peter Lorre. Sydney Greenstreet. Mary Astor. Ward Bond. Rhineheart had seen it nine, maybe ten times. "Where's it playing?" he asked.

"At the Vogue. On Lexington Road. Two bucks admission. My treat," McGraw said.

"I'll buy the popcorn," Rhineheart said.

It was after midnight when the movie ended. It had rained and the streets were wet and glistening. Rhineheart and McGraw went to the White Castle, ate hamburgers, drank coffee, and talked about their favorite scenes. Then he took McGraw home and drove back to his apartment.

Rhineheart got a beer from the refrigerator and stretched out on the couch with a paperback mystery. Maybe he could pick up some tips on deduction.

He was halfway through the first chapter when the telephone rang. He picked up the phone and a woman's voice said, "Mr. Rhineheart?"

"Yeah?"

The words came rushing across the line—"Carl Walsh wants to see you. He wants to talk to you. Meet him at the Downs. The backside. The tack room, Barn 24B. Half an hour." The line went abruptly dead.

Rhineheart put the phone down. He got to his feet. What the fuck was going on? He walked over to the window and pulled back the blinds. What was he looking out the window for? The call was some kind of setup. Clearly. The thing to do was ignore it. Read the book. Go to sleep.

He walked over to the closet, reached up, and took down the shoulder holster. He strapped it on. Why was he putting on his holster? He wasn't going anyplace. Only a fool would go out there.

He walked over and opened the top drawer of the desk. His gun, a Colt Python, was lying there. He picked it up and checked the chamber. It was loaded. He stuck it in the holster. Stupid. Dumb. It was beyond dumb.

He put on his coat and headed out the door.

* * *

Rhineheart stepped out of the shadows between the
barns. He looked down the shed row, which was lighted
by a line of naked light bulbs. There was no one in
sight. At the end of barn 24B a faint fan of light
streamed out of the tack room window. It was quiet,
except for an occasional stir and nicker from behind the
stall doors.

Behind him was the gap to the backstretch and the
clocker's stand, a squat two-story cinder-block building.
Ahead, and on both sides, were horse barns.

As he headed down the shed row toward the tack
room, Rhineheart looked around. The surrounding barns
seemed deserted. Something was wrong. During Derby
Week the place was supposed to be top-heavy with security. Where were all the rent-a-cops? Now that he thought
about it, it had been a shade too easy to get into the
stable area. He had climbed the fence on Longfield Avenue, and had seen no one on his trip across the backside.

He stopped and took out his gun and held it at his
side, pointed at the ground. Nothing was going to happen. But it was better to be ready. He was moving forward when he heard the crack of a weapon, and the light
bulb over his head exploded with a loud *thwock,* spray-
ing him with fragments of glass. The second shot
slammed into the closed upper half of a stall door. Not
waiting for a third, Rhineheart hit the ground, which was
wet and straw-covered, propped himself on both elbows,
and squeezed off two quick shots in the general direction
—the barn behind and to his left—from which the fire
had come.

There was no return fire. He thought he saw somebody
—a man's shape—moving away in the darkness. He
couldn't be sure.

He scrambled to his feet and ran toward the backstretch.
Ahead, a shadowy figure vaulted the rail and ran up the
track toward the clubhouse turn, disappearing from Rhineheart's view when it passed behind the clocker's stand.
Rhineheart jogged up to the rail. The figure had vanished
into the darkness.

Behind him, tack room lights were coming on, voices

were being raised. It was time to split, but as he turned to leave he looked up, his eye caught by the sight, in the distance, across the track, of the famous twin spires. Outlined against the night sky, they loomed ominously up above the track and the surrounding landscape. There was something sinister about the way they stood there high above everything, the whole mess.

TWELVE

The next morning Rhineheart woke at nine, threw on some sweats, drove over to Bellarmine, ran twenty laps around the track, and drove back home. He showered, shaved, and got dressed. Tan slacks. A navy blazer. White shirt. Button-down collar. No tie. He put his gun in the shoulder holster and strapped it on. He drank three cups of coffee and read the morning paper, which had an article about the mysterious slaying of a racetrack worker whose body had been found Sunday morning in a Dixie Highway motel. Rhineheart washed the cup out in the sink, went out to the Maverick, and drove down to his office.

It was located on Main Street in downtown Louisville, down the block from the Kentucky Center for the Arts and the Humana Building. It was on the fifth floor of a hundred-year-old building that was being renovated floor by floor. By the time the renovators reached Rhineheart's floor he was sure he wouldn't be able to afford the rent.

The sign on the door said MICHAEL J. RHINEHEART, PRIVATE INVESTIGATOR. Inside was one large square room with a twelve-foot ceiling, a scarred hardwood floor, and six tall narrow windows that overlooked the intersection of Seventh and Main.

Rhineheart had picked up the furniture here and there. A beat-up leather couch. A battered old filing cabinet. Several chairs. A couple of desks. His was an old, worn walnut rolltop with a lot of pigeonholes. McGraw's desk was smaller, a gray steel job that sat in the corner.

McGraw was seated behind it, hunched over an old Royal Standard. Rhineheart watched her hunt and peck for a moment. On her job application she had stated that she could type sixty words per minute.

Rhineheart said, "I thought *I* was the world's worst typist."

"You were wrong," McGraw snapped.

"Good mood, huh?"

"Here's the mail." She handed him a stack of letters, which he dropped on his desk.

"I get any calls?"

"Someone named Patty Dubois. Said she was Public Relations Director of Cresthill Farms. Wants you to call her back. I left the number on your desk. Oh, I almost forgot. A Karen Simpson called. She says you have her number."

Rhineheart smiled . . . enigmatically, he hoped.

"Who's Karen Simpson?" McGraw asked.

"Material witness," he said.

Rhineheart opened the second drawer of his desk, where he kept a box of ammunition. He took his weapon out of the holster and began loading it.

McGraw gave the Python a bad look. "What's *that?*"

"What do you mean, what's that? You never saw a gun before?"

"Do you— Are you . . . going to . . . ?"

"Relax," Rhineheart said. "I'm just loading it."

"What happens after you load it?"

"I put it back in the holster. Like this." He reholstered the weapon.

McGraw said, "I'm not into guns."

"Neither am I."

"How come you're carrying one, then?"

"I may need it," he said. "Things are starting to get a little funny." He sat down and put his feet up on the desk.

"What do you mean *funny?*"

"I got shot at last night."

"You got *shot at* last night?"

Rhineheart nodded. "As a matter of fact," he said, "it might be a good idea if you stayed away from the office for

A gray-haired housekeeper answered the door. She led him through a small foyer and along a wide hallway to a medium-sized oak-paneled room that seemed to be a combination den and office. The carpet was thick enough to mow. English hunt prints hung on the walls. The windows were covered by thick, pewter-colored drapes. A huge antique partners' desk sat in front of a marble fireplace. The chairs were leather and commodious.

Rhineheart was checking out one of the prints—Dapple Gray Fording the Creek—when Howard Taggert strode into the room. Taggert was a tall, gaunt man with bushy eyebrows, a long, leathery face, and a grizzled iron gray mustache. Sixty. Maybe sixty-five. And tough, Rhineheart decided.

Taggert was wearing a tweed sport coat with leather elbow patches, a turtleneck sweater, and khaki slacks tucked into a pair of dirty work boots. A pipe angled out from one corner of his mouth.

He gave Rhineheart's hand a brisk shake. "Good morning. I'm Howard Taggert. What can I do for you?"

"My name's Rhineheart. I'm a private investigator."

Taggert raised one eyebrow skeptically.

Rhineheart took out his wallet and showed Taggert the license.

Taggert didn't look overly impressed. "You're a private investigator. What do you want with me?"

"I'd like to ask you a few questions."

"About what?"

"One of your employees was found dead in the Red Wind motel this weekend."

Taggert nodded. "Felix Sanchez. He was an exercise rider. According to my stable foreman, he was a good hand. I talked to the detective assigned to the case yesterday. His name is Wilson. He interviewed a number of my people. He didn't say anything about any private investigator working on the case."

"I don't work with the police," Rhineheart said. "I operate on my own."

Taggert's face seemed to lengthen.

"What's your interest in Sanchez?" he asked Rhineheart.

"It has to do with a case I'm working on," Rhineheart said. "You happen to know if Felix Sanchez knew Carl Walsh?"

"Who?"

"Carl Walsh. You know who Carl Walsh is, don't you?"

Taggert frowned and nodded. "Yes, I know him. He used to work for me. I fired him a couple of years ago. He was responsible for ending the racing career of a filly of mine. Through sheer carelessness. He's lucky I didn't kill him. I understand he works for Cresthill Farms now. For"—Taggert spoke the words with evident distaste— "Duke Kingston. And no, I don't have any idea if Sanchez knew Walsh. Why? What does Walsh have to do with anything?"

"He's disappeared."

Taggert took the pipe out of his mouth. "Disappeared?"

"Walsh left his apartment on Wednesday night. He didn't show up for work the next day. No one has seen him since."

Taggert was silent for a moment. Then he said, "I don't understand why you've come to see me."

Rhineheart shrugged. "I'm not sure why I came to you, myself. I guess I was hoping you might be able to tell me something about Walsh, something that might help me get some idea where he is."

"The only thing I can tell you about Walsh is that he is like most other people I encounter these days—feckless and irresponsible. No discipline. No sense of responsibility. No standards. As far as where he might be, I have no idea. He worked for me for two years. That's the extent of my knowledge of the man."

"You were seen talking to him on Tuesday, the day before he disappeared."

Taggert's jaw clenched. "I was, huh?" His voice rose. "What do you mean, I was *seen?*"

"I mean someone saw you," Rhineheart said.

"What someone?" Taggert fixed Rhineheart with a stern look. "Am I being spied upon by somebody?"

"Take it easy," Rhineheart suggested.

"Don't tell me to take it easy," Taggert declared. "Who

in the hell are you to tell me to take it easy? I want to know who's spying on me."

"As far as I know," Rhineheart said, "no one's spying on you. Someone saw you talking to Carl Walsh on Wednesday. That's all."

"That's all, huh?"

"Yeah."

"Well, that's not all as far as I'm concerned," Taggert said. He thrust his face close to Rhineheart's. "Who are you working for?" he demanded.

"I can't tell you that," Rhineheart said.

"Is it *Duke Kingston?*" Taggert's voice grew shrill with anger. It didn't look as if he was a big fan of Duke Kingston.

"What difference does it make who I work for?"

"It makes a difference to me," Taggert said. "Answer me, are you working for Duke Kingston?"

"None of your fucking business," Rhineheart said. He was tired of messing with the temperamental old bastard. Taggert needed punching, but he was too old to hit. It was too bad Farnsworth wasn't along. Farnsworth was Taggert's age and same general build. Farnsworth might be able to handle the old dude, Rhineheart thought. Maybe.

"It's Duke Kingston, isn't it? You're working for him, aren't you? He hired you to come over here and harass me, didn't he?"

Rhineheart decided to give it one more shot. The old man was goofy, but maybe if he talked softly and politely and was nice . . .

"Look—" Rhineheart began.

Taggert's right arm shot out in the direction of the hallway, a long, trembling index finger extended. "Out," he shouted in a loud, quavery voice. "Out!"

"I thought maybe we—"

"Out! Get out of my house now."

The gray-haired housekeeper appeared in the doorway. She had a stolid look on her face, as if she was used to such outbursts. Rhineheart shrugged and walked over to her. As she escorted him toward the front door, he thought of a couple of smart-ass remarks he might have made. *I've been kicked out of better houses than this one*, for instance.

While not strictly true—it was probably the nicest house he'd ever been kicked out of—it had a certain ring to it. The thing was, he doubted if he could have got it in over the sound of Taggert's voice.

THIRTEEN

Rhineheart drove west on River Road. He was headed back downtown. Off to the right, the big Ohio streamed along placidly. Across the river thickets of trees lined the Indiana shoreline. He flipped on the radio and twisted the dial until he found something he could stand listening to. Aretha Franklin.

He had just passed the Water Tower, a tall white columnlike structure that was some kind of historic landmark, when he spotted the tail. A red Camaro. Three cars back. A big guy with a beard sat behind the wheel. A bald-headed guy rode shotgun.

Rhineheart stayed on River Road. As he drew closer to the city the landscape changed, turned ugly. Sand and gravel companies bordered the river. Gas and petroleum tanks squatted on both sides of the road.

He turned left onto Third Street, took another left on Market, a right on First, and swung up the ramp to the North–South Expressway. The Camaro stayed a couple of car lengths back. He maneuvered the Maverick into the center lane and hit the gas to open up a little daylight between his car and the Camaro. Traffic was fairly light. There were cars ahead and on both sides. Nothing directly behind him.

The Camaro was fifty yards back and in the same lane when Rhineheart stomped on the brakes. The Maverick came to a squealing, shuddering halt. Cars, horns bleating, rushed past on both sides. In the rearview mirror he watched the Camaro swerve into the right lane. As it slid past, tires squealing, Rhineheart leaned forward and got the license number. It was a Jefferson County plate—HJL 356.

He looked up—into the rearview mirror. A mammoth semi, an eighteen-wheeler, was bearing down on the Maverick, its horn bellowing loudly. He jacked the gearshift down into first and squealed away. He continued down the expressway for a few miles, but the Camaro was nowhere to be seen.

He got off the expressway at Lee and took Second Street back downtown. He parked in a lot at the corner of Third and Jefferson and walked across the street. It was a seedy, squalid block occupied by porno shops and massage parlors and topless bars. Rhineheart stepped into a narrow open doorway that adjoined the Peep Show movie theater. He climbed a rickety set of stairs to the second floor and pushed open a frosted door whose faded letters read F RNS ORTH D TEC IV AG NCY.

Farnsworth was seated behind an old, beat-up desk. He had his feet up and was asleep in his chair, his head thrown back, mouth open, revealing a set of badly fitted dentures. He was wearing a shiny blue pinstripe suit and a white shirt with a frayed collar. A thin black tie was knotted tightly around his neck. On his feet he wore old-timey suede-on-leather, gray-on-black, two-tone shoes. There was a hole in each sole.

Rhineheart sat down on a hard wooden chair and cleared his throat loudly.

The old man came awake with a snort, dropped his feet to the floor, sat up straight, and tried to look alert. He ran thin shaky fingers through the sparse tobacco-colored hair that was combed straight back from his forehead. His face was long and narrow, his features a collection of sharp angles and severe planes. He squinted at Rhineheart. His eyes were like slits.

"What can I do for you?" The voice was thin and high-pitched.

He doesn't remember me, Rhineheart thought. "It's me," Rhineheart said.

"Who?"

"Rhineheart."

"Rhineheart?" Farnsworth said.

"You don't remember me," Rhineheart said.

"What do you mean I don't remember you?" Farnsworth said, peering at him. "You nuts or something? How could I forget the Kid?"

Rhineheart smiled. The Kid was what Farnsworth had always called him. Back when they had worked together —in the early '70s. Rhineheart had been a young street kid just out of the army who wanted to become a private investigator. Farnsworth had given him his first job, had taught him the business. Farnsworth had been an *old* bastard even then. Old—but sharp.

"It's been a little while," Farnsworth said.

It had been years since they had seen each other. "Too long," Rhineheart said.

"How ya doing, kid?"

"Fine. How about you, old man?"

"I'm not doing too bad," Farnsworth said.

"How's business?" Rhineheart asked. It was a dumb question. One look around the room told him how Farnsworth's business was doing.

But Farnsworth said, "It ain't bad. I get all the night watchman work I want. Every once in a while I get a *real* case—a divorce, or a runaway, or something. With that and my social security"—he shrugged—"I'm doing okay." He gestured at the room. "This place is a dump, but the rent is cheap, and you can look out the window, Rhineheart, and see the city. There ain't a suburb or a shopping center for miles."

Farnsworth, Rhineheart remembered, had a thing about the suburbs and the country. He didn't like wide open spaces or any neighborhood that didn't have sidewalks. The best private eyes, he claimed, were city boys who had grown up on the crowded urban streets.

"What about you?" Farnsworth said. "You still in the trade?"

The trade. Once you were in the trade, Farnsworth used to say, it got in your blood and you were *always* in the trade.

Rhineheart shrugged. "What else is there?"

Farnsworth smiled. "You working for somebody now?" he asked. "One of them big outfits?"

"I got a little office over on Main Street," Rhineheart said.

Farnsworth nodded. "You was never the type to work for somebody else. You always had a hard time following orders. Even from me. You were good, though. A little reckless, but a good operative. You still reckless, kid?"

"I was followed on the way over here." He told Farnsworth about the incident on the expressway. The old man cackled and slapped his palm down on his knee and said, "God damn, boy, that was a nice piece of driving. It sounds like you're in the middle of something hairy."

Rhineheart nodded. "Yeah, it's getting kind of complicated. That's why I came to see you. I need some help," he said. "I need another operative. I figured you might be able to handle it. If you got the time, that is."

Farnsworth didn't say anything for a moment. He looked stunned by the offer. He reached up and smoothed out his tie. Then he withdrew a large white handkerchief from his coat pocket, unfolded it several times, buried his nose in the folds, and cut loose with several loud honks. He inspected the handkerchief, refolded it, and replaced it in his pocket. Then he cleared his throat and said, "I'm a little bit busy, but I think maybe I can help you. Fill me in, kid."

Rhineheart filled him in. He told Farnsworth about the case—from the first meeting with Kate Sullivan to the shooting at the racetrack the night before. When he was done telling it, Farnsworth sat back in his chair, and let out a low whistle.

"Jesus," Farnsworth said, "you got a real lulu here. Missing people. Derby horses. A dead Spic. A syringe. Mafia goombahs. Socialities. It's enough to make your head spin."

"I'm going to concentrate on Walsh," Rhineheart said. "See if I can find him. I'd like you to see if you can locate his wife and talk to her. She might know where he is. She's a nurse's aide, works at Saint Anthony's." He dug out the slip of paper he'd found in Walsh's garbage. "Maybe you can make some sense out of this. I found it at Walsh's apartment. You're the ace when it comes to deciphering puzzles."

Farnsworth smoothed out the piece of paper and looked at it. "I'll see what I can do, kid."

"As far as the rest of it goes, you're on your own. Play it any way you want to. Do whatever you need to do, whatever you think's right. You're on the payroll as of this afternoon. You need an advance?"

"Well . . ."

Rhineheart pulled out some bills, handed Farnsworth two fifties.

"I'll keep a strict account, kid."

Rhineheart nodded. "I'll see you later, old man."

FOURTEEN

It was after three when Rhineheart got back to his office. McGraw was on her way out the door, but she stopped long enough to tell him that Kate Sullivan had phoned and left a message to call her as soon as he got in. The number was on his desk. No one else had called and McGraw had to hurry. She had a date. A hot one. With an attorney who worked in the prosecutor's office.

"Where's he taking you?"

"Dining and dancing," McGraw said.

"Does he know how much you eat?"

"Kiss my ass, Rhineheart." McGraw stomped out, slamming the door behind her.

Rhineheart dialed Kate Sullivan's number. She came on the phone, and they exchanged greetings. She asked Rhineheart how the case was going. He told her it was going okay. She asked if there had been any new developments. Rhineheart said no, nothing worth talking about.

"You're not exactly forthcoming, are you, Michael?"

Forthcoming? What the hell was that? Rhineheart remembered that the Kingstons' maid had begged his pardon. Everyone in the case, it seemed, was well spoken. Even the servants. Maybe they were all conspiring to use words that weren't in his vocabulary.

"I come forth," Rhineheart said, "when the occasion warrants." He wasn't sure what that meant, but it sounded good.

Kate laughed. "Very well said, Michael."

"Do you know who Howard Taggert is?" Rhineheart asked.

"Yes, of course. River City Stud. Calabrate."

"There's a chance he's involved in this."

"What makes you say that?"

"It's too complicated to explain over the phone. I'll tell you about it when I see you."

"Let's get together soon," Kate Sullivan said.

"Soon," Rhineheart promised.

She asked Rhineheart to call her if he found out anything else. He promised her he would, and after she hung up, he called the Motor Vehicles Bureau and asked to speak to L. T. Dewhurst.

L.T. was a computer programmer. For a twenty-dollar bill, L.T. could get you the name and address of any license-plate holder in the state. Rhineheart gave L.T. the number of the red Camaro. L.T. excused himself, was gone thirty seconds, then came back on the line with the news that the Camaro's license number was registered in the name of Executive Transport, Inc., a car-leasing agency whose offices were in the 3900 block of Shelbyville Road.

"A car-leasing agency?"

"I just push the keys, Rhineheart. I got no control over what comes out."

"I'll send you a check, L.T."

Before Rhineheart left the office, he called Marvin Greene's number.

"Yeah?"

"Marvin, this is your old buddy, Rhineheart."

Marvin didn't say anything for a moment, then in a fakey friendly voice, he said, "Hey, Rhineheart. How you doing? What do you need?"

"I want to talk to you, Marvin."

"So talk."

"In person. Private."

"What's this about?"

"I'll meet you somewhere," Rhineheart said. "You still hang around the Kitty Kat Club?"

"No," Marvin said too quickly.

"Where then?"

"You know where the Backstretch Lounge is?"

"Yeah." It was on Berry Boulevard. Near the track.

"I'll be there around seven."

"Wait for me," Rhineheart said.

The customer relations representative for Executive Transport, Inc., thought Rhineheart resembled her favorite movie actor. "No kidding," she kept saying. "You look just like him."

The customer relations rep's name was Diana Martindale. She was a good-looking woman in her mid-thirties, blonde, blue-eyed, with a sexy smile and a nice body. She had fine-looking thighs. She was sitting at her desk with her skirt hiked up. Rhineheart sat across from her, trying not to stare too deliberately at her thighs.

"Hasn't anyone ever told you how much you look like him?" Diana Martindale asked. "You've got the same kind of nose and chin."

"Bent and big?"

"Exactly."

"You're just saying that to get next to me, aren't you?"

"You're not married, are you?"

Rhineheart looked at her. "No," he said, "I'm not married."

"Are you going with anybody?"

"Nobody'll have me," he said.

She laughed.

"About these lease records . . ." he said. Rhineheart had spent the past half hour trying to get a look at the lease invoices.

"They're supposed to be confidential."

Rhineheart said. "And I promise to keep them that way. You tell me who rented this license number"—he pushed a slip of paper across the desk—"and it'll go no further."

Diane Martindale looked around the room to make sure none of the other people in the office were watching her. She opened a steel box on her desk, flipped through the card file, and pulled out an invoice card, which she handed to Rhineheart.

The invoice was made out to the Capitol Investment Corp., with an address on East Broadway. There was a scribbled signature at the bottom, but Rhineheart couldn't make it out.

"You look disappointed," she said.

"I am." He handed her the card, and glanced at his watch. It was quarter after four, too late to make it to the tax assessor's office and check out Capitol Investment Corp. before they closed. Well, the assessor's office would be there tomorrow.

He stood up and smiled at Diane Martindale. "You've been very helpful," he said.

She returned the smile and handed him a slip of paper. "My address and telephone number," she said. "Call me anytime."

"Sure," Rhineheart said, but he didn't really think so. She was a good-looking woman with a nice body, but so were Wanda Jean and Karen Simpson and five or six other women he knew. He had all the one-night ladies he needed. He stuck the slip of paper in his pocket, and walked out of the place, feeling old and tired and a little lonely.

FIFTEEN

Rhineheart drove out to the track and caught the last two races. He bet the winner of the feature, and in the last, he had twenty dollars on the winning exacta, a 4 and 8 combination that paid $112.00. He left the track with over a thousand in his kick. He felt better. Hitting the exacta was like an omen. Maybe it meant he was going to find Carl Walsh, solve the case, be a winner for a change.

Rhineheart ate dinner at Trattori's, an Italian restaurant on Bardstown Road. He had Veal Parmesan and spaghetti and drank two glasses of wine. After dinner he drove over to the Backstretch.

Marvin was sitting at a table in the rear. Marvin had a receding hairline and a potbelly. He wore a Derby Fever T-shirt and Bermuda shorts. He was peeling the label on his beer bottle. He peered at Rhineheart through thick, wire-rimmed glasses.

"Hello, Rhineheart."

"You nervous, Marvin?"

"What do you mean?"

"You seem a little nervous."

"What'd ya want to see me about, Rhineheart?"

"I'm working on this case," Rhineheart said. "I come across your name. I thought maybe you could help me out."

"In what way?"

"In an information way."

"I ain't no snitch, Rhineheart."

"You owe me two or three favors, Marvin."

"Sure, of course. I'm just saying I ain't nobody's snitch, Rhineheart. Favor's a different thing."

"Who bets with you, Marvin?"

"Hey, come on now, that's confidential stuff. Like *your* job. You don't go around talking about your clients, do you?"

"Does Howard Taggert bet with you?"

Marvin shook his head. "I'm too small-time for someone like Taggert. If he bets, he bets personally with the Big Man."

"Corrati?"

Marvin looked over his shoulder, then around the room. Finally, he nodded.

"What about Duke Kingston?"

"Out of my league also."

"Does he bet?"

"I hear he does." He paused. "Heavy."

"What else do you hear about him?"

"I don't hear nothing else. I make it a point not to hear about people like that. They carry too much weight for guys like me."

"Tell me about Carl Walsh."

"Who?"

"You fuck with me, Marvin," Rhineheart said, "and I'll throw you through the window there."

Marvin held up a hand. "Easy, easy. Okay, Walsh bets with me. He's into me for two dimes. I cut him off, told him to get the money up by next week. I ain't heard from him for a couple of days."

"Since when?"

"Last week. I ain't sure."

"Think."

"Early last week. Monday or Tuesday. He says he'll have something for me this week."

Rhineheart put a twenty on the table and stood up. "Thanks, Marvin."

Marvin snatched up the bill. "No sweat."

"I find out you been bullshitting me, I'll be back."

* * *

John Hughes's address was in the two-thousand block of Brownsboro Road. A rectangular complex of squat, pale green, pseudo-Spanish-style apartments.

Rhineheart parked in the lot, climbed an outside stairway to the second floor of B Building. The sounds of a party—music, voices, laughter—drifted out from behind Hughes's door.

Rhineheart knocked, and from inside, a slurred voice yelled, "Come in!"

He pushed the door open and walked into a large, square room filled with people. There was a buffet table on one side of the room and a well-stocked bar on the other. The furniture was heavy-looking, Mediterranean.

The wall at the far end of the room was a large glass window. The drapes were open, and through the glass, you could see row after row of squat, pale green buildings. It was a hell of a view, Rhineheart thought. If you looked out at it long enough you'd probably get brain damage.

Most of the guests looked as if they were already suffering from it. Rhineheart asked one of them, a spiky-haired platinum blonde wearing oversized shades, if she knew where John Hughes was.

"What do you want *him* for?" she asked Rhineheart. "Why don't you hang around and talk to me?"

"I like your hair, but this is business, babe. Show me Hughes, will you?"

She frowned and pointed to a tall thin man with a guardsman's mustache who stood near the buffet table. Rhineheart walked over and introduced himself.

Hughes was dressed in a tan safari shirt and dark brown slacks and he was holding a glass full of whiskey in one hand. Scotch, from the smell that drifted Rhineheart's way.

He reminded Rhineheart of the British actor, Peter O'Toole. His angular English features had a smeared look to them. He appeared to be about three-quarters smashed.

He brushed a shock of thick brown hair back from his forehead, and squinted, bleary-eyed, at Rhineheart.

"What did you say your name was?"

"Rhineheart."

"Rhineheart? I've heard that name somewhere. What is it you want, old man?"

"I'd like to talk to you for a few minutes."

"You're not one of those bloody *Sports Illustrated* people, are you?"

"No."

"No," he said. "Of course you're not." He nodded in the direction of the bar. "Have a drink, old man."

"No thanks."

"I'm the host of this bleeding party. It's not polite to refuse one's host."

"I'm not a polite person," Rhineheart said.

Hughes took a big swallow of his drink. Over the rim of his glass, he peered nearsightedly at Rhineheart. "I say, old man, do we know each other?"

"I don't think so, no."

"No. Of course not. Well, Mr.—what did you say your name was?"

"Rhineheart."

"Rhineheart, of course." Hughes swayed to the left. 'Well, Mr. Rhineheart, what can I do for you?"

"You could answer some questions."

Hughes smiled, a loose, silly, drunken smile. "I know who you are," he said, pointing a finger at Rhineheart. "You're the chap who's looking for Carl Walsh. The private"—Hughes hiccuped—"eye."

"That's me."

Hughes waved a hand. "Fire away, old man. Hope I can be of some help."

"When was the last time you saw Walsh?"

Hughes wrinkled up his forehead. "Let me think. Sometime Wednesday afternoon. I popped by the barn. Walsh was in the tack room with a couple of the other lads. I think they were playing cards."

"He seem any different than usual?"

"Not that I can recall."

"What can you tell me about Walsh?"

"How do you mean?"

"I'm trying," Rhineheart said, "to get an idea of what kind of person he was."

Hughes took another swallow of his drink. His voice took on a light slur. Walsh, he said, was a pleasant enough chap. Did what he was told. Came to work on time usually.

Hughes understood that Walsh liked his drink and liked to chase the ladies, but who didn't?

"Did he gamble?" Rhineheart asked.

"I really don't know."

"Walsh get along with his fellow employees?"

"I suppose so."

"Last week," Rhineheart said, "you and Walsh had an argument behind the barn. What was it about?"

Hughes flashed a stiff smile at Rhineheart. "To tell you the truth, old man, I don't really remember what it concerned. I probably had to dress him down for something he did—or more likely, something he didn't do. Walsh is not the only lad I've ever had to tongue lash. It's something that comes with the head trainer's job, I'm afraid."

"You think of any reason why Walsh'd leave so abruptly?" Rhineheart asked.

"Obviously, you're not very well acquainted with race-trackers, Mr. Rhineheart. They're gypsies. They come and go as they please. At the drop of a hat." Hughes drained his drink.

Rhineheart looked around the room. People stood around in little groups, drinks in hand. They were partying hard, as if it were a job. The music—some heavy-metal shit—had been turned up a couple of decibels and someone had laid out a line of coke on the coffee table. The spiky-haired blonde was bent over the table.

It was time to split, Rhineheart decided. He wasn't getting anywhere with Hughes anyway. He made it a point to thank Hughes courteously, excused himself, and made his way out of the place. None of the partygoers seemed to notice his departure.

On the way home he stopped at O'Brien's. The place was almost empty. It was Wanda Jean's night off. McGraw was out on her date, having a good time, no doubt. For a moment he considered calling Kate Sullivan. Then he realized she was probably spending the night with her husband and her kids. He ordered a drink and sat on a stool at the bar.

He had a couple of doubles and Sam, the bartender, came over and leaned on the bar top and asked Rhineheart how he was doing. Sam was in his sixties and had been around the block a time or two. Rhineheart tried to get him to talk about the old days before TV, when everything, life itself, seemed to have more meaning than it did now and everyone was nicer and money wasn't everything and the Kentucky Derby was the only horse race in the world and people from all over came to Louisville to see it.

But all Sam wanted to talk about was basketball. He asked Rhineheart who was going to have the best team. U. of K.? U. of L.? Indiana?

Rhineheart shrugged. He couldn't get interested in roundball until December. He wanted Sam to tell him about the Brown Hotel and the celebrities who stayed there back in the forties and about all the great races, but he just sat there and listened to the old man talk about seven footers and power forwards until closing time.

Just before Rhineheart got up to leave, a dumpy woman in a print dress who had been sitting at one of the tables walked over to him. She put her hand on his arm, and in a voice full of sympathy, said, "You had a bad day at the track, didn't you, son?"

"Actually," Rhineheart said, "I won."

"Don't kid me," the woman said. "I can always tell a loser when I see one." She patted him on the shoulder. "Well, maybe you'll do better tomorrow," she said. But there was no conviction in her voice. She gave him a bleary smile and shuffled out the front door.

Rhineheart looked at himself in the mirror behind the bar. The woman was right: he had loser written all over him.

SIXTEEN

When Rhineheart woke up the next morning the sun was coming up. He threw on some jeans and a windbreaker and drove out to the Downs. He parked the car on Longfield Avenue, showed his pass to the gate guard, and walked over to the backstretch.

The area around the clocker's stand was crowded with racetrackers and press people. The track was filled with horses working out. Rhineheart spotted an old friend, a small-time trainer named Murphy, sitting on the rail. Murphy made room for him.

"How are ya, Rhineheart?"

"I'm okay, Murph."

"Come to see the workouts?"

"I come to see Royal Dancer. He on the track?"

Murphy nodded. "Somewhere."

"Do me a favor," Rhineheart said. "Point him out to me when he comes by."

"Sure."

Murphy gestured at the crowd around the gap. "You ever see anything like this? It's a goddamn circus, ain't it?"

Looking around, Rhineheart agreed. In the crowd he noticed a familiar figure: Howard Taggert. Taggert was talking to a short, broad-shouldered man wearing a wide-brimmed Stetson.

"Who's the guy in the hat?" Rhineheart asked Murphy.

"Which one?"

"Talking to Taggert."

"That's the vet, Doc Gilmore," Murphy said.

DR. G.

Gilmore. The name sounded familiar. "How come I know that name, Murph?"

"He's the one the Arkansas racing commission brought up on charges a few years back. Made all the papers."

For doping horses, Rhineheart remembered. "Whatever happened?"

Murphy shrugged. "He got acquitted."

"He Taggert's vet?"

Murphy nodded, then pointed to a lean chestnut rounding the clubhouse turn, a helmeted exercise rider on its back.

"Royal Dancer," he said.

Royal Dancer's stride was fluid and easy. He was, Rhineheart saw, a good-looking colt.

"What kind of horse is he, Murph?"

Murphy shrugged. "He's a stakes winner. Got all kinds of speed."

"He got any kind of chance?"

"In the Derby?" Murphy shook his head. "I doubt it. Hasn't run enough, for one thing. He win that race back in January in Florida big, then didn't run again until last month in Arkansas. He had a big lead and quit. Run seventh, eighth, I forget. He didn't show me a lot. Plus, I don't like the way Hughes trains that Cresthill stock. Works 'em too hard in the mornings, you ask me."

"His owner seems to think he's got a chance," Rhineheart said.

Murphy shrugged. "Lots of dreams floating around out here. Lot of dreamers."

"You know Kingston?"

"I see him around," Murphy said. "We don't exactly move on the same social levels."

"What about Taggert?"

"Same thing. Why are you asking about them two?"

"No special reason. Just interested."

"You on a . . . case, or something?"

"Something."

"Word around here is that Taggert and Kingston can't stand each other's guts."

"How come?"

Murphy shrugged. "There's some bad blood between them. Goes back in the past. Something to do with a mare one of them owned."

"What do you think about Taggert's horse?"

"Calabrate? He'll be one of the favorites. Got a real shot, run a big race in the Wood. Personally though, I like this here horse—" Murphy pointed at a dark gray whose rider was standing straight up in his stirrups. "Blustering."

Murphy began to explain why he liked Blustering, but Rhineheart wasn't listening. He was looking around for Taggert and Gilmore. They had disappeared.

Rhineheart was walking back to his car when he noticed a flurry of activity around Barn 41, the building where all the Derby horses were stabled.

Eight to ten reporters and photographers were grouped around a figure he recognized.

Duke Kingston.

Kingston looked as if he were posing for a cover of Gentleman's Quarterly. He wore a cashmere sportcoat and linen trousers and a scarf tied around his neck. He was being interviewed and a cameraman with a minicam on his shoulder was filming the scene.

Rhineheart was too far away to be noticed, but close enough to overhear. The perfect position for a private eye.

"Where's Royal Dancer right now, Mr. Kingston?" a reporter asked.

Kingston gestured in the direction of the backstretch. "He's out on the track, working out."

"How's he coming up to the race?" someone asked.

"Supah," Kingston said. "Just supah."

"How about you, sir?"

"I'm doing okay, too."

Everyone laughed.

"What kind of chance do you think he has on Saturday?"

"Just a small one," Kingston said. "Everything depends on the pace. If it's slow and Dancer gets out there and Julio gives him the sort of ride he's capable of, why then we think we might have a chance to steal some part of the purse money, maybe get on the board anyway."

"Don't you really mean, Mr. Kingston, that you might have a chance to win?"

"Of course."

"How do you feel about your horse being a long shot?"

"I'm glad Royal Dancer can't read the odds board."

"Is Dancer the best three-year-old colt you've ever had, Mr. Kingston?"

Kingston shook his head. "I don't know. I guess we'll see about that come Saturday, won't we?"

"Can your colt go a mile and a quarter, Mr. Kingston?"

"We think he can, yes. Again though, we won't know for sure until after the race is over."

"Mr. Kingston, your horse is known for his early speed. Aren't you afraid that when the time comes he'll have nothing left for the stretch run?"

"Son, when you been in the racing game as long as I have, you either stop being afraid of all the possible consequences, or else you get out of the business."

"Mr. Kingston, can you tell us something about—"

Rhineheart spun on his heel and headed for the exit, shaking his head with a kind of sneaking admiration. Kingston was something. A high-level bullshitter. He had handled one question after another deftly and easily. His voice and his gestures were assured and decisive. Whatever else he was, Rhineheart thought, the man had presence, style.

Rhineheart drove home and went back to sleep for a few hours. He woke at noon, showered, shaved, and dressed. He drank a cup of coffee and read the morning paper. He was on the editorial page and his second cup when the telephone rang.

It was Karen Simpson.

"I thought maybe you might like to come over and interrogate me some more."

"I'm going to be busy today, babe. But I'll try to make it."

"You promise?"

"Cross my heart and hope to die."

She giggled and hung up. Rhineheart dialed the office. McGraw answered the phone.

"Rhineheart Investigations. McGraw speaking."

"Morning, McGraw."

"*Morning!* Are you serious? It's twelve-thirty. Don't tell me you're just now getting up. You ought to be ashamed of yourself. No self-respecting private eye would sleep as late as you do, Rhineheart."

The best way to handle McGraw's lectures, Rhineheart had discovered, was to ignore them.

"I get any calls?"

"Negative. What time are you coming in?"

"Later on," Rhineheart said.

"I love how specific you are. Precise."

"You going to be there?"

"I don't know. Maybe. I've got a class at four."

McGraw was into adult education courses. "Sociology?"

"Tai kwan do."

"That shit won't do you any good in a street fight," Rhineheart said. "The thing you want to do if someone messes with you is pick up something—a bottle, a brick, whatever it takes."

"Is that the Michael P. Rhineheart theory of self-defense?"

"It's no theory. It's the real thing."

"You going to see Jessica Kingston again?"

"Yeah."

"What's she want to see you about?"

"No idea."

"Well, be careful."

"I'm always careful," Rhineheart said.

"She's out of your league, Rhineheart."

"Thanks for the advice, McGraw."

"And Rhineheart?"

"Huh?"

"Let her pick up the check. She can afford it."

"Good-bye, McGraw."

SEVENTEEN

"I think my husband's considering offering you a job, Mr. Rhineheart. He was very impressed with you."

Rhineheart took a sip of his drink. Jessica Kingston, who sat across the table, was wearing a light-colored summer dress. She looked terrific.

They were in the bar off the lobby of the Seelbach. It was an old-timey and elegant hotel, the kind of place that had a doorman who wore top hat and tails. F. Scott Fitzgerald had written about the Seelbach. Gatsby had taken Daisy to a dance there.

"I saw him this morning," Rhineheart said.

"Duke?"

"Out at the track. He was holding a press conference. He handled himself very well."

"Duke can be quite charming."

"I'll bet." Rhineheart lit a cigarette. "What kind of a job?"

Jessica Kingston shook her head. "I have no idea. Something in your line, I should think. Maybe he wants you to spy on me. That'd be quite a task, Mr. Rhineheart. You'd have to follow me around, go where I go, see who I see. You'd have to stick close to me."

"Sounds pretty good."

"What a nice thing to say. Are you flirting with me, Mr. Rhineheart?"

"I guess I am. Do you mind?"

Jessica Kingston shook her head. "I'm rather enjoying it."

Be cool, Rhineheart told himself. Remember who she is and who you are. Don't make any dumb moves.

"Actually," he said, "what your husband's probably looking for is another security consultant. Like Mr. Borchek."

Jessica Kingston laughed merrily. "Perhaps you're right."

"And I've already got a job."

"Duke thinks he can buy everybody who walks in the door," she said. "Apparently, he was wrong about you."

"What did you want to see me about, Mrs. Kingston?"

She raised an eyebrow. "As always, you get straight to the point, don't you?"

He shrugged. "Why not?"

She said, "Why not, indeed. I asked you here, Mr. Rhineheart, because I have some information for you. It concerns Cresthill Farms and possibly Carl Walsh. It may be of some help to you in your investigation." She paused. "How much do you know about thoroughbreds, Mr. Rhineheart?"

"Not much."

"Do you know what foal papers are?"

"No."

Jessica Kingston removed a manila envelope from her purse and withdrew from it a neatly folded piece of paper. She unfolded the paper and handed it to Rhineheart. "This is the foal registration certificate on a Cresthill mare who died a few years back. I brought it with me to show you what foal papers look like."

It was an official-looking document with scrolled borders, approximately the same size and shape (9 by 9, rectangular) as a share of IBM he had once caught a fleeting glimpse of. The front side of the document read:

**THE JOCKEY CLUB
CERTIFICATE
OF FOAL REGISTRATION**

This is to certify that the bay filly named SEA PRINCESS
foaled SEP 21, 1964   by SEAFARER
Out of FISHGAL   by PRINCE SURF
is duly registered by the Jockey Club.
Marks: Small star—forehead. Crescent-shaped scar— right forefoot. Discoloration—right hind pastern.
Issued to: CRESTHILL FARMS
Bred by: CHARLES "DUKE" KINGSTON
Foaled in: KENTUCKY

Rhineheart turned the paper over. The reverse side was divided into two sections, an official record of races won on the North American continent, and a space for recording all transfers and sales of the registered animal.

While he looked it over Jessica Kingston filled him in on the significance of foal certificates. Every thoroughbred in North America had one. They were issued by the Jockey Club in New York. Racetracks used foal papers to identify the different horses stabled on the grounds. Foal papers had to be on file in the racing secretary's office before a horse could run at a particular track. This rule applied to all horses and all races. If a horse's foal papers were missing he would not be allowed to race.

Rhineheart looked up from the document.

She nodded. "Royal Dancer's foal certificate is missing, Mr. Rhineheart. It was discovered missing last Wednesday, the same day that Carl Walsh disappeared."

"This mean that Royal Dancer's not going to be allowed to run in the Derby?"

She shook her head. No, she said, fortunately there was a procedure for getting copies of missing foal papers. It was complicated and expensive and somewhat time-consuming. It involved long-distance communication between the Jockey Club in New York, and the racing secretary's office here, and thank God, that was being taken care of. Nevertheless, the original certificate was missing, and she had decided to tell Rhineheart about it on one condition. He had to promise not to tell anyone about the missing certificate, and above all not let her husband know that he knew about it.

"He wants to keep it a secret?"

She nodded. "From everyone he can. He's afraid that the press might find out about it, and that Cresthill could receive some adverse publicity."

"How would a missing foal certificate result in bad publicity?"

"In Duke's view any publicity about the racing stable that isn't favorable, is adverse."

"You said the paper's been gone since Wednesday. You think Walsh took it?"

"I don't know. I *do* know that Carl Walsh had access to it. The paper was in John Hughes's car on Wednesday. He was getting ready to bring it over to the racing secretary's office. The car was parked by the barn. Walsh was in the vicinity."

Walsh, Rhineheart remembered, had been seen talking to Howard Taggert the day before. Did that mean that Taggert might have something to do with the missing paper?

"Any chance that Howard Taggert's involved?"

Jessica Kingston looked surprised. "Howard Taggert?"

"He and your husband are enemies, aren't they?"

She nodded reluctantly. "Yes, I suppose so, but—"

"Tell me why they hate each other."

"It's a long complicated story, and even I don't know all the details. Duke and Howard Taggert were partners once. They owned a broodmare together: Somethinglovely. She's the dam of Royal Dancer. She also happens to be the foundation mare on which Cresthill Farms has built its racing stable. Taggert claims Duke swindled him out of the mare. Duke says it was an honest transaction. They don't speak to each other anymore. Taggert hates Duke and everything connected to Cresthill Farms, including me, I suppose. But I have no idea if he would stoop to stealing foal papers." She signaled the waitress. "Perhaps when you find Mr. Walsh you might ask him."

If I find him, Rhineheart thought.

The waitress came over to the table. Jessica Kingston ordered a second martini. The waitress, who had red hair, asked Rhineheart if he wanted another drink, or anything else. He said no thanks. She asked Rhineheart if he was sure. When he said he was, she looked disappointed. After she left, Jessica Kingston said, "The waitress seems quite interested in you, Mr. Rhineheart."

He shrugged. "She's probably wondering what I'm doing in here. This place is a little too nice for private eye types." In truth, Rhineheart was pretty much wondering the same thing. What was he doing here on a spring afternoon in the plush bar of a grand old hotel sitting across the table from a rich and beautiful woman? He had a case to solve, and he should have been out in the streets, detecting, running down leads, taking care of business.

"I haven't asked you about the investigation yet. Are you any closer to finding Carl Walsh?"

Rhineheart shrugged. "That's hard to say. I've been followed. I got shot at the other night, and everyone's been lying to me. So I must be doing something right."

"You got shot at?"

"Uh-huh."

"What did you do when they shot at you?"

"Shot back."

"You carry a gun then?"

Rhineheart nodded.

"May I see it?"

"I guess so," Rhineheart said. He took the weapon out of his shoulder holster and handed it to her. Her slim well-manicured fingers encircled the grip.

"It's big, isn't it?" she said. "What kind of a gun is it?"

"Colt Python. Six shots."

"Is it powerful?"

He shrugged. "It's a .357 Magnum. It does the job."

"I bet it does," she said. She handed it back to him carefully. Their eyes met. She smiled.

He put the gun back in his holster. I better get the hell out of here, he thought, before I make a bad move. He stood up.

"One more thing, Mr. Rhineheart." Jessica Kingston took a white envelope out of her purse and handed it to Rhineheart. "It's an invitation to my party," she said. "Thursday at nine. At Cresthill. I'd very much like you to come."

"Sure," Rhineheart said. "It'd be a pleasure. Can I bring someone?"

"Of course."

"Her name is McGraw."

"Bring anyone you like, Mr. Rhineheart."

"If I run across those foal papers, Mrs. Kingston, I'll let you know."

"I'd be grateful, Mr. Rhineheart."

"Good afternoon."

"Take care, Mr. Rhineheart."

This is ridiculous, Rhineheart thought, as he turned and walked out of the place. He was supposed to be the tough, sophisticated private eye, and his heart was booming in his chest like a goddamn kid on his first day at school.

EIGHTEEN

It was midafternoon when Rhineheart got back to his office. McGraw had lunch—hamburger, fries, milk shake—spread across her desk.

"I thought you were into health food," Rhineheart said.

"Big Macs aren't healthy?"

"That shit'll rot your gut."

"How nicely put."

"How was your date last night?"

McGraw made a face. "Don't ask."

"That bad, huh?"

McGraw nodded. "It's the reason I'm stuffing myself with this junk. I'm a tragedy eater. I eat when I'm depressed."

"I get any calls?"

"One. From someone named Farnsworth. He said he'd call back. He called me 'girlie.'"

"Be nice to him," Rhineheart said. "He's the guy I told you about from the old days. He's working for us."

"How was lunch with Jessica Kingston?"

"It wasn't bad."

McGraw gave Rhineheart a look. "You really go for her, don't you?"

He shrugged. "She's okay."

Rhineheart sorted through the mail on his desk. There was a check from Channel 6. He gave it to McGraw. "Deposit that when you get a chance, and write yourself a check for last week's pay."

ed and fifty known." She looked him
g through a at up recently? I'm talking
rt coat that so."
had curly door. "I'll be back."
a summer s class," McGraw said. "You
ered by a r?"
mes. Cor-
ok on his at the Vogue tonight?"
who was man. I got to find a missing per-
Rhine- there's some missing papers."
his feet
to get it later. I don't have time now. And I
.38 in be going to the movies." Rhineheart
, then stopped. "What's playing?"
nute I
ward G. and John Garfield. Ida Lupino.
Ha. ael Curtiz. From a script by Robert Ros-

ne-thirty."
ake it," he said, "I'll call you."

nty Tax Assessor's office was located on Fifth
o of Market. Business and corporation files were
kept e second floor. The office was spacious and well
lit. Neat rows of filing cabinets stood behind a long
wooden counter.

A sallow middle-aged man in a brown bow tie brought
Rhineheart the Capitol Holding file. Capitol Investment
was incorporated on June 9, 1979. Its principal business
was real estate and stock market investment. Its corporate
offices were located at 312 Broadway. The president of
Capitol Investment was Howard Taggert. The vice president was Harrison Gilmore. They were the principal of-
ficers of the company that leased the car that had been
tailing him.

It was almost five when Rhineheart got back to the office. He unlocked the door and stepped inside.

Two people were there, waiting for him.

One was Angelo Corrati. All three hundr[ed]
pounds of him was seated on the couch, leafi[ng]
magazine. He was dressed in a camel-hair sp[ort]
looked to Rhineheart like a size sixty. Corrat[i]
black hair and a face as round and as smooth a[s the]
moon. His eyes, little black buttons, were co[vered]
pair of lightly tinted glasses with thick, steel fra[mes. Cor-]
rati glanced up from the magazine with a bored l[ook on his]
face.

The other guy was muscle, a big black guy [who was]
seated in Rhineheart's chair with his feet up o[n Rhine-]
heart's desk. He considered telling the guy to get [his feet]
off the desk, but he decided it wasn't a good ide[a to get]
nasty with someone who was pointing a Walther PK[K in]
your direction.

Maybe humor was the right approach. "For a m[inute I]
thought you two were Dean and Sammy."

In a flat humorless voice, the black guy said, "Ha [ha.]
The man's a comedian."

Corrati said, "You're Rhineheart."

Rhineheart nodded.

Corrati pointed to a chair.

"Sit."

What the hell. Rhineheart sat down.

Corrati said, "You know me, you know I'm a man w[ho]
doesn't fuck around with a lot of bullshit small talk. I heard
about you. You're a private cop. I hear you been around some
places looking for somebody. I hear you stop in my club the
other night, talk to an employee, ask her some questions,
show her a picture of somebody. That right?"

"Yeah."

"Couple days later you go see a friend of mine, an associate. You ask him a lot of fucking questions ain't none of
your business. So what's the deal? What's going on? Who
you looking for? Who you working for? Why you doing it
in my places of business?"

"You got me mixed up with someone else," Rhineheart
said. "Some loose-mouthed snitch you know, or something. My name is Rhineheart. I thought you said you'd
heard about me."

The corners of Corrati's mouth tightened in what Rhineheart decided was a smile. "I heard that about you. People tell me you're a stand-up guy. Don't take no shit. That's admirable. That's truly fucking admirable. I admire balls in a person. On the other hand, I can get your knees broken for you in five seconds. You see what I'm saying? Basically, I mean?"

"I see your point," Rhineheart said, "but if you heard about me, then you know you can break my knees, and I won't tell you who I'm working for. If I did, I'd be out of business tomorrow."

Corrati leaned back in the couch. The leather creaked under the weight. "What if I told you that I know who you're working for and who you're looking for and why you're looking for him and the whole thing?"

"I'd believe it," Rhineheart said. "I heard that about you. You keep yourself informed."

"You're fucking right I do. I keep my fingers on the buttons. Anything that concerns me. Or affects my business. Which is why I, uh, come down here to see you today. I like to stay on top of things. You understand where I'm coming from on that?"

"Sure."

"So how's your investigation going?" Corrati asked.

Rhineheart shrugged. "Not too good."

"You didn't find the person you're looking for, did you?"

"No."

"No," Corrati said, "and I don't think you will, either."

"What do you mean?" Rhineheart asked.

"I'm just talking," Corrati said. "What do I know? Maybe he left town. He owes my associate some money." The couch creaked again as he leaned forward. "Let's talk some business, Rhineheart. One businessman to another."

"Now I *know* you got me mixed up with someone else."

"I'm going to make you a deal," Corrati said. "Your part of the bargain is you forget looking for the Walsh kid. That's a waste of time, anyway."

"What's your part of the bargain?" Rhineheart was dumb enough to ask.

Corrati smiled. "My part is I don't have you squashed like a fucking bug."

Rhineheart didn't say anything. What was there to say?

"You don't have to say yes or no right now, Rhineheart. Sleep on it. Think it over. Get back to me. In the next day or two. Or else I'll get back to you." He pushed himself up out of the couch and walked over to the door. He moved as if he were wading through mud.

The black guy took his feet off Rhineheart's desk and stood up. He kept the Walther pointed at Rhineheart as he went over to the door and opened it for Corrati. Corrati walked out into the hall, followed by the black guy, who pulled the door shut behind them.

NINETEEN

Rhineheart, for some reason, didn't feel like eating supper. He drove home. As he walked in, the phone was ringing.

"Yeah?"

"Kid."

Farnsworth. "How you doing, old man?"

"Not too bad. I found out a couple of things."

"Yeah?"

"Walsh's wife. You're right. She works at Saint Anthony's. Maternity ward. Eleven to seven. Except she ain't been to work since Friday. Called in sick. They haven't heard from her since. Woman in personnel let me peek at her file. She's from Detroit." Farnsworth pronounced it *Dee*-troit. "Called up her parents. Pretended to be a hospital administrator searching for a reliable nurse's aide at a good salary. Wanted to know how to locate her. They gave me the Parkland Arms address and telephone number. Said Rhonda was down here living with her husband. They said they hadn't talked to her for a few days, but they didn't sound worried. They seemed on the level."

"Anything else?"

"Tomorrow, I'm going to have lunch with a couple of the gals she works with, see if they might have any idea where she's gone."

"Sounds good."

"Also, I think I figured out who that Dr. G. is on the piece of paper you found."

"The name you came up with wasn't Harrison Gilmore, was it?"

"I see you been working, too, huh?" He cleared his throat. "One more item."

"What's that?"

"I found out who Lancelot is. Lancelot's a $10,000 claimer. Win the second race at Keeneland three weeks ago Tuesday. Paid a sixty-eight-dollar bill."

"Lancelot's a *horse?*"

"And guess who owns him?"

"Howard Taggert."

"Wrong. You get two more guesses."

"Quit fucking around, old man."

"The vet."

"Gilmore?"

"And John Hughes is listed as trainer. And, kid, some funny stuff there. I got that day's past performances and there's no way the horse looks like he can win. He run terrible his last five races. He's moving *up* not down in class and he beats a field of classier horses by five lengths. You talk about reversal of form."

"What are you saying? You think it was a boat ride?"

"I'm saying I think it was a funny race. Maybe they put something funny in the horse."

Maybe so, Rhineheart thought. Maybe that explained the syringe.

"You did good, old man."

"Not bad, huh? For an old guy."

"Keep at it. I got a lot of shit to tell you about. I'll call you tomorrow. We'll compare notes."

"Good enough, kid. I'll see you then."

Rhineheart hung up the phone, and went over and stretched out on the couch. He thought about the visit from Corrati and the missing foal papers and the information about Lancelot. What did it all mean? And more important, how was it going to help him find Carl Walsh?

The phone started to ring. He got up, walked over, and picked it up.

"Yeah?"

"I want to speak to Mr. Rhineheart." The voice of a young woman, nervous.

"This is Rhineheart."

"This is Tammy Shea. The girl who works at the Hideaway. Remember me?"

"I remember you, babe."

"The other night you said you wanted to help. Is that the truth?"

"Yeah."

"I've got to talk to somebody. Can I trust you?"

"You can trust me, yeah."

"It's about . . . something Carl told me. I don't know whether to call the police or not."

"The police?"

"I think someone followed me home tonight."

"Tammy, where do you live?"

"The Regal Arms. Brook and Hill. Apartment 33."

"Keep the door locked. I'll be there in fifteen minutes."

Traffic on the expressway was heavy. Twenty minutes later Rhineheart pulled up in front of the Regal Arms, an old yellow-brick apartment building that had been built back in the twenties and had seen better days.

He double-parked in the street and took the stairs to the third floor. Apartment 33 was the second last door on the right, near the end of an unlighted hallway. He pressed the buzzer. No one answered. He hit the buzzer again. Nothing. So he tried the knob. The door swung open. Uh-oh . . .

Rhineheart took out his gun, slipped off the safety, and stepped inside, into a small narrow living room. The furniture was dismal and cheap. On the right there was an even smaller dining room and a short hallway that led to the bedroom. That's where he found Tammy Shea. She was lying in the middle of a large double bed. She was dressed in jeans and a green top, resting on her back, one arm flung above her head. Her eyes were shut, and in repose, her face, which was framed by her dark hair, was a picture of innocence and peace and youth. She might have been sleeping.

The only trouble with the picture was she was dead.

There was a small caliber—probably .22, Rhineheart thought—bullet hole in her left temple. A thin line of fresh blood ran from the wound down her cheek to form a round red spot on the white pillow where her head rested.

Rhineheart felt for the pulse in her throat, but it was a useless gesture. Lately, it seemed, he had been making a lot of useless gestures.

In my line of work, Rhineheart thought, you see too many dead bodies, and too much blood. And the worst thing is, you tend to get used to it. He stood there looking down at the dead girl and tried to summon up some feeling, some sense of sorrow or anguish for her death. But it was no use. He had met her once, but she was a stranger to him. It wasn't that her death didn't matter. It was that his mind was operating on another frequency. He was wondering what to do next—call the police, search the apartment, or look for the killer who might still be in the vicinity?

He must have been concentrating too hard. He didn't hear the noise behind him until it was too late. A heavy object collided with the back of his head. His brain seemed to explode, then fill with darkness, and he felt his body sinking slowly to the floor.

Rhineheart came to with his face pressed against a thin, worn carpet. He opened his eyes. A wave of pain rippled through his head. He pushed himself up from the floor, got to his hands and knees, and then, slowly, to his feet.

Far off somewhere, in the distance, he could hear a faint high-pitched whine. He looked around. Everything seemed blurred; then gradually the dimensions of the room began to take shape. He checked his watch: he'd been out ten minutes.

In the bedroom nothing had changed. Tammy Shea's corpse was still lying across the bed. The whine was getting louder, and he realized it was the sound of a siren a few blocks away but drawing closer.

Someone had set him up. His car, he remembered, was double-parked out front. He staggered out of the bedroom, and made his way out of the apartment, down the hallway, down the stairs, and out the door to the street. He slid in behind the wheel and wheeled the Maverick around the corner. He was halfway down the block when he looked in the rearview mirror and saw a Louisville Police cruiser roar past the intersection, its siren screaming, its blue lights flashing and whirling.

* * *

Rhineheart drove over to the emergency room at Suburban. An Oriental doctor sewed up his head, bandaged it, gave him a shot of something, and told him it would be best if he stayed in the hospital overnight. The nurse told him he had a serious concussion and that if he wasn't careful it could lead to brain damage.

"Thanks for your help," Rhineheart said.

She nodded and handed him a bill for $85.00. He paid it at the cashier's desk and went out to the Maverick and drove home. He drank a beer, and tried to watch a late movie, but his head hurt too badly. He undressed and lay down in bed. He didn't think about the case or the dead girl. He started thinking about the meeting at the hotel with Jessica Kingston, replaying it over in his mind. It was stupid. The private eye and the socialite. It was dumb, he knew, to keep thinking about her. But he couldn't help it.

TWENTY

Wednesday morning Rhineheart woke at ten. His head felt as if a little man had been inside there stomping on his brain cells all night long. He got out of bed carefully, dressed, and fixed himself a pot of coffee. The telephone rang while it was brewing.

The caller introduced himself as Calvin C. Clark. Rhineheart recognized the name. It belonged to a well-known attorney, a lobbyist and dealer in political favors. Calvin Clark was a power broker who ran with senators and governors and people like that. His office was in Frankfort, the state capital.

Mr. Clark said that he wanted to discuss a business proposition with Rhineheart. The proposition was one that he doubted Rhineheart could pass up once its terms were made clear. He couldn't go into any of the details over the phone, but he wondered if Rhineheart couldn't spare him some time later this afternoon and come to his office.

Rhineheart's answer was that he was kind of busy, but would try to make it. Clark thanked him and hung up. The shit, Rhineheart thought, was starting to pile up. It was turning out to be some kind of a case. He was hanging around horse farms, meeting rich folk, getting invited to swanky parties. The movers and the shakers of the earth were calling him on the phone and talking about business propositions. Rhineheart wondered what it was the man really wanted. It might be both interesting and worthwhile to find out.

Rhineheart dialed the number of Yellow Cab. He asked the man who answered what cab company had green cabs.

"What am I?" the man said. "An information service?"

"This is Chuck Fisher," Rhineheart said, *"Agent* Fisher of the IRS. Connect me to your supervisor."

"I'm sorry, Agent Fisher. I musta got out of the wrong side of the bed this morning. Green cabs'd be Independent. Want their address?" The man gave Rhineheart the address. It was on Forty-fourth Street in the West End.

"Thanks," Rhineheart said. "You may have saved yourself an audit."

Rhineheart was pouring milk into his coffee when the phone started ringing again.

He walked into the front room and picked it up. "Yeah?"

"You're going to have to work on your telephone etiquette, Rhineheart."

There was only one person with a voice that deep and gravelly. Sergeant Katz.

"What do you want, Katz?"

"Get your ass down here, Rhineheart. I want you to meet someone."

"Who?"

"Carl Walsh."

"What are you talking about, Katz? You got Carl Walsh down at headquarters?"

"Actually, he's over at University. In the basement."

The basement of University Hospital was where the police morgue was located.

"I'll see you there in fifteen minutes," Rhineheart said.

"Make it ten," replied Katz.

A body lay on a cart with wheels. It was covered by a sheet. Katz pulled back the sheet. The face was swollen and discolored, but Rhineheart could see it was the face of the guy in the photograph that Kate Sullivan had given him. There was no doubt of that. He turned his head away. He had seen enough dead bodies lately.

Katz put the sheet back over the body and walked out of the room. Rhineheart followed him into the white-tiled hall. Katz dug a pack of Camels out of his coat pocket, lit a cigarette, coughed, stared at Rhineheart. He didn't say anything.

The ball was in Rhineheart's court. "How'd he die?"

"He drowned," Katz said.

"Drowned?"

"That's what Willingham says." Willingham was the county coroner. "They pulled Walsh's car, an old VW, out of the river about six o'clock this morning. Near a boat dock. Walsh was behind the wheel. Lots of alcohol in his blood: .19, something like that. Willingham's going to rule it was an accident." Katz looked at Rhineheart. "Walsh had a large contusion on the back of his head, but that's not inconsistent with the accident ruling."

Rhineheart was silent for a moment. Then he said, "Were there any personal effects?"

Katz smiled. "Wallet. Car keys."

"What was in the wallet?"

"Driver's license. ID. Couple of bucks."

"That all?"

"What else would there be?"

"I don't know," Rhineheart said.

"According to the ID," Katz said, "Walsh was a race-tracker, worked for some stable out at the Downs, lived in the South End. He's got a wife, but we haven't been able to get in touch with her. That's all we know about him." He flipped his cigarette onto the floor where it lay smoldering. "Unless you got something to tell us, peeper."

Rhineheart shook his head. "I don't know anything more than you do."

"Bullshit," snapped Katz. "Why were you looking for him?"

He was going to have to tell Katz something. The question was how much. "Walsh has been missing since last Thursday."

"Missing from where?"

"From home. From work. I was hired to find him."

"By who?"

Rhineheart had to smile. Katz was probably the only person he'd talked to recently who spoke worse English than he did. "Actually," he said, "that's *whom*. The correct way to say that, Katz, is 'by whom.'"

"Get fucked, Rhineheart. I want to know who hired you."

"I can't tell you that, Katz. It would"—Rhineheart searched for a word—"uh, *breach* the relationship between my client and me."

"'Fuck you talking about?"

"I'm talking about the legal relationship," Rhineheart said, "between a client and a private investigator."

"You got your shit mixed up, Rhineheart. What you're talking about is the confidential relationship between a lawyer and his client. It don't apply to private eyes."

"Unless the lawyer *is* the client."

"Is that what you're telling me, peep? A lawyer is your client?"

Rhineheart nodded. "Yeah." The nuns at Saint Joseph's, Rhineheart remembered, said that whenever you told a lie you got a spot on your soul.

"Bullshit," Katz said.

"I swear to God, Katz."

Katz took out another Camel, jabbed it between his lips, lit it, spat out some smoke, coughed. "I don't give a shit if your client is a fucking judge. I want to know what all this is about."

"No you don't," Rhineheart said. "You just *think* you do. When I tell you the names of some of the people involved in this, you're going to say I wish you hadn't told me that, Rhineheart."

"Quit fucking around, peeper. I want some names. Now."

"What happens if I don't give you any?"

"I take you downtown," Katz said. "I book you on some bullshit charge—withholding evidence or something. I ask the prosecuting attorney who owes me a couple of favors to ask the judge who owes *him* a couple of favors to suspend your license for a six-month period and to set your bond up there in the five-figure range."

"I thought we were friends, Katz."

Katz looked at Rhineheart as if Rhineheart were crazy. "What the fuck has friends got to do with it?"

Rhineheart shrugged. "Have it your own way. You want names? How about Duke Kingston?"

Katz's mouth dropped open. "Duke Kingston?"

Rhineheart nodded.

"You're bullshitting me. Kingston's way out of your league."

"Take another look at Walsh's ID. See if he doesn't work for Cresthill Farms."

Katz sucked on his cigarette, coughed. He looked a little worried. Katz was a tough cop, but he was also, Rhineheart knew, leery of people with power and influence. He had pursued an investigation too far once, the story went, come too close to a powerful politician, and had been burned for it. The politician had made a phone call. Katz had been busted, transferred to a desk job. It had taken him a couple of years to make it back to homicide.

"There's media people involved also," Rhineheart said.

"What do you mean? What media people?"

"Local TV news people."

"Shit," Katz spat out.

"It's strictly a simple missing-person thing so far," Rhineheart said. "And it looks like the missing person's no longer missing. If it turns out to be anything else, Katz, you'll be the first person I'll call."

Katz gave him a bad look. "I find out you been bullshitting me about this, peeper, it's your ass."

Rhineheart resisted the temptation to smile. Katz was trying to save a little face. He tossed his cigarette on the floor and started to walk away.

"Hey, Katz."

Katz stopped. "Huh?"

"Can I get a peek at Walsh's wallet?"

"That's illegal," Katz said. "The wallet's official police property."

"Yeah," Rhineheart said. "I know."

Katz looked at Rhineheart. Then he shrugged. "Come downtown and see me tomorrow. We'll talk about it." He turned and started to leave, then he stopped.

"Hey, peeper."

"Huh?"

He nodded at Rhineheart's bandaged head. "What happened?"

"I banged it against something," Rhineheart said.

Katz snickered. "Yeah. Like what? A blackjack."

"How'd you guess?"

"You keep taking them blows to your head, peep, what brain you got's gonna get mushy."

"Won't be nobody's big loss," Rhineheart said.

"Keep in touch," Katz said on his way down the hall.

TWENTY-ONE

Rhineheart called Kate Sullivan at the TV station from a pay phone in the hospital lobby.

"I've got some news, Kate. We need to meet. Now."

"Baskerville's?"

"Ten minutes."

Kate was sitting in one of the booths. Rhineheart slid in across from her and waved the waitress away.

"What happened to your head?" she said.

"I hit it against something," Rhineheart said.

"You said you had some news."

"Carl Walsh is dead."

She looked shocked. "Dead?"

Rhineheart nodded. "Police pulled his body out of the Ohio this morning. They say he was drunk, drove his car into the river."

"An accident?"

"That's what the police think."

"What do *you* think, Michael?"

"I think he was murdered. I think somebody poured booze down his throat and pushed his car into the river to make it look like an accident. I don't know why he was killed. Maybe he knew something that somebody didn't want him to know. Something that was going to 'blow the town wide open,' like he told you. I don't know who killed him either."

"Do you have any suspicions?"

"A few, yeah."

"Would you mind sharing them with me?"

Rhineheart shook his head. "Better not."

"I'm still your employer, am I not?"

Rhineheart shrugged. "I don't know. Are you? Walsh has been found. In that respect, my job is done."

"Don't you intend to find out who killed him?"

Rhineheart smiled. "I was thinking about it, yeah."

"Good," Kate said. "Because that's precisely what I want you to do. I want to remain your client, Michael. I feel sure the station will back me in this. I want you to find out why Carl Walsh was killed, Michael, and who did it."

"There's a new player in the game," Rhineheart said. "You know who Angelo Corrati is?"

She nodded. "He's a local bookmaker, isn't he?"

"He's *the* bookmaker. He handles all the heavy action locally. He stopped by my office yesterday afternoon. He said he was looking for Carl Walsh, too. Walsh owed him some money. Corrati wants me to stop looking for Walsh. He offered me something in return."

"What?"

"My life."

Kate Sullivan seemed shocked. "He threatened you?"

"Yeah."

"Were you frightened?"

"I don't frighten. I can be bribed," Rhineheart said, "but I don't scare."

Kate Sullivan looked puzzled. "You can be *bribed?*"

"Just kidding."

"You're angry at me," she said.

"I'm not angry at you."

"Yes, you are."

"You're right," Rhineheart said. "I am."

"I'm sorry I said that, Michael. Please don't be angry with me."

"All right," Rhineheart said, "but you're going to have to be cool. We may be getting into some funny stuff here. Things could get wild. In that kind of situation you have to hang tight and have your shit together."

"I'll do my best," she said.

"Remember when we were kids," Rhineheart said, "the nuns would catch us talking and try to get us to tell on each other?"

"I remember."

"We never snitched on each other, Kate. We stuck to-gether. That's the kind of thing I'm talking about."

"The only trouble with that scenario, Michael, is that it isn't true. I was afraid of the nuns. And when they threat-ened me, I told on you every chance I got."

Rhineheart laughed. "You did, didn't you?" He shrugged. "Well, this time try to do better, okay?"

"Okay."

He stood up. "I'll be in touch with you when I find out something."

"You'll keep me informed about any new developments, won't you?"

"Don't worry," Rhineheart said.

"And, Michael, be careful please."

"Don't worry, babe."

Independent Cab was on Forty-fourth near Broadway, a storefront, squeezed between a pool room and a laundro-mat. Inside, a fat black lady wearing a headset sat behind an old-fashioned switchboard.

"Help you?"

"I need to talk to the cabbie who picked up a fare at the Parkland Arms. On Southern Parkway. Last Wednesday night. Around nine-thirty."

"What are you—a cop or something?"

"Private eye."

"Hmmmf." She made a sound, flipped open a logbook, studied it a minute, then closed it. "That'd be J. T. Smith. He was the only driver on duty last Wednesday."

"Where do I find Mr. Smith?"

"He don't come on duty 'til eight tonight. Then you can catch him at the airport. His stand in front of the Eastern exit."

"Thanks."

"Hey, you ever look for runaway husbands?"

"Not this week," Rhineheart said. "Call me up next week though, and I may be available."

"I may do that," she said, "but truth is, for right now, I'm sorta glad he's gone."

* * *

Rhineheart stopped at a street pay phone and made two calls. The first was to Farnsworth, to bring him up to date: Tammy Shea, the missing foal papers, the visit from Corrati, the scene at the morgue, and the call from Clark.

"Jesus," the old man said, "you've been busier than hell. Can we meet later?"

"O'Brien's. Seven o'clock."

"I'll look for you, kid."

Rhineheart's second call was to his office.

McGraw answered. "Rhineheart Investigations."

In the background Rhineheart could hear the office radio. It was tuned to some "easy listening" station. A string section was going to town on "Moon River."

"You actually listen to shit like that?" he asked McGraw.

"Up your wazoo, Rhineheart."

"You ought to be ashamed of the way you talk to your employer, McGraw."

"I am."

He told McGraw about Carl Walsh and his visit to the morgue.

"Oh Christ, that's rough," she said. "What does that mean? Is the case over?"

"In some ways, it's just starting. Look, I want you to find me Dr. Harrison Gilmore's address. Home and business."

"You want me to do that now, or later?"

"Later," Rhineheart said. "I get any calls?"

"Three. All from your so-called material witness, Karen Simpson."

"If she calls again, tell her I'll get back to her."

"Where you going?"

"Frankfort."

"To see the governor?"

"Close. I ought to be back in town around five-thirty, six o'clock."

"Take it easy, Rhineheart."

"Don't worry."

TWENTY-TWO

It took Rhineheart an hour and twenty minutes to drive to Frankfort and find Calvin Clark's law firm. It was located in a restored Victorian mansion near the Old Capitol. A trim and tanned secretary let him in, led him down a tiled hallway, pushed open a door, and ushered him into an oak-paneled office.

A tall, white-haired gentleman in a dark suit stood up and greeted him. "Good morning, I'm Calvin Clark. Have a seat, please. Can I have my secretary get you anything? Coffee? A drink?"

"No thanks."

"Mr. Rhineheart, I assume you're aware of the fact that in addition to being the principal legal counsel for the Kentucky Horse Owners Association, I'm also a member of the board of directors of a Lexington-based firm known as Thoroughbred Security, Inc."

"No," Rhineheart said, "I'm not aware of any of that."

"Well, it's a fact, Mr. Rhineheart. By the way, I'd like to offer you my congratulations on a successful investigation."

"What investigation are you talking about?"

"Why, the one concerning the fellow who worked for Cresthill Farms. I understand from the police that you were quite diligent in your search for him. Unfortunately, you didn't find him in time to prevent a rather—from what I've been able to gather—horrible accident. But you can hardly be blamed for that. Personally, I think you did a yeoman job."

Rhineheart didn't say anything. It was no surprise that Clark knew about Walsh's death already. The rich and powerful didn't get that way by being dumb or staying uninformed.

Charles Clark smiled. "You keep your own counsel. I admire that."

Rhineheart sat still, said nothing, waited.

Clark cleared his throat. "We may as well get down to business. At Thoroughbred Security we're always head hunting, so to speak, for a few good men. For the past several years we've been following your career, Mr. Rhineheart."

My *career?* Rhineheart thought. Was the man serious?

"Some of the publicity you've received hasn't been altogether favorable, but all in all we think you're an impressive man, Mr. Rhineheart. We like your style. I've been authorized by the board to offer you a position with the firm."

"A position?" Rhineheart repeated. "You mean a job?"

"If you prefer."

"What kind of a job?"

"Vice president of our Field Operations Branch."

"Vice president?"

"It's an executive level position."

"What does a vice president of a Field Operations Branch do?" Rhineheart asked.

"Well, for one thing, he oversees and supervises our guard unit personnel, three shifts, one hundred and fifty men who patrol the farms serviced by our company. And let me say this, Mr. Rhineheart, almost every large well-known thoroughbred horse farm is protected by Thoroughbred Security."

Rhineheart wondered if that included Cresthill Farms and River City Stud, but decided not to ask. Instead, he asked Clark what other responsibilities the vice president had.

"Among other things," Clark replied, "he would supervise and train the personal security consultants that travel with the owners and protect them during public appearances."

Like Borchek.

"The new field operations VP," Clark went on, "would also develop and plan additional security for the stabling areas at various racetracks. In this connection the position would, naturally, entail some travel."

"What's a job like that pay?"

Clark couldn't hold back a grin. "It has a starting salary of $65,000 a year, plus, of course, a generous expense account, the full package, naturally, of health and medical benefits, a stock-option plan, a company car of your choice, and yearly bonuses that are substantial."

Substantial. If he accepted, would that make him a person of substance? Sixty-five thousand was a pretty good-sized bribe. Someone wanted him in their pocket, out of the way. Who? Kingston? Taggert? Gilmore? Clark? What were they afraid he was going to stumble across?

"What do you think, Mr. Rhineheart?"

"It sounds pretty good," Rhineheart said.

"Frankly, in my opinion it's the kind of position a man could hardly afford to pass up." He cleared his throat again. He looked at his watch. "I hope you'll let me have the pleasure of telling my people that you've accepted our offer."

"I don't think so."

Mr. Clark looked disappointed. "I'd hate to see you let this opportunity go by, Mr. Rhineheart. It's not the kind of job that's going to stay available for very long. Already we're looking at some other applicants. If you turn it down someone else will snap it up."

"I understand."

Clark cleared his throat again. "I have something here," he said, "that might help you clarify your thoughts on the matter." He leaned across the desk and handed Rhineheart a check. It was a certified cashier's check for $25,000 and was drawn on the First National Bank of Kentucky. "The sum you see there represents an incentive bonus should you decide to sign a contract to work for Thoroughbred Security before Derby Day."

"Derby Day?"

"We need to fill the position immediately."

"And, of course," Rhineheart said, "if I take your job, I'd have to close my agency."

"You simply wouldn't have the time for a private practice, Mr. Rhineheart."

"What about the cases I'm working on?"

"I'm sure you could make some arrangements with another agency to take them over."

Rhineheart held the check in his hands. He could keep it as a souvenir, show it to McGraw, frame it on the wall: My Biggest Bribe. On the other hand, maybe he'd cash it and take the fucking job. After all, $65,000 wasn't bad money. And the job sounded pretty nice. You probably had to take some shit. But for $65,000 . . .

He put the check on Clark's desk. "I don't know who you represent, Counselor," Rhineheart said, "but tell them I can't take your job."

"Why not?"

"Simple. I already got one."

It was late in the afternoon when Rhinehcart pulled into an empty parking space in front of his apartment building. He let himself in, got a can of beer from the refrigerator, switched on the TV, and stretched out on the couch to see if he could catch Kate Sullivan on the early news.

She appeared on the newscast a couple of minutes after it started in a taped segment that dealt with the board of aldermen's attempt to annex an unincorporated city that adjoined Louisville. It was a boring, colorless story but Kate delivered it with style. She seemed to be pretty good at her job. Rhineheart watched the program a few minutes longer. When they switched away to live coverage of one of the Derby Festival events, a steamboat race between *The Belle of Louisville* and *The Delta Queen*, he lost interest and turned off the set.

He went into the kitchen and threw some ham and some cheese between two slices of bread. He spread some Mr. Mustard over the ham. The Gourmet Dick. He ate the sandwich and drank another beer and thought about the $65,000 a year. It was a lot of money. It took character to turn it down. Character or ignorance. He wasn't sure which.

He finished off the sandwich and was washing out the coffee cup in the sink when the phone began to ring. He walked into the front room and picked it up.

"Rhineheart."

"It's me." McGraw.

"How's it going, babe?"

"Okay. Listen, I got Gilmore's address for you." She read it aloud. Rhineheart wrote it down.

"Babe, I appreciate it."

"What are you going to do tonight?"

"I got to meet Farnsworth. Then I'm going over and talk to a cabdriver."

"Want some company?"

"Not this evening," he said. "I want you to save yourself for rougher times—like tomorrow night."

"What's tomorrow night?"

"What do you mean, what's tomorrow night? The big Derby party at Cresthill Farms."

"Oh my God. Are we going to that?"

"Me and you, babe."

"Oh God, I don't have anything to wear."

"Don't worry about it," Rhineheart said. "I don't either."

"Is that supposed to make me feel better?"

"Look at it this way, McGraw, it doesn't make any difference if we dress wrong. Neither one of us knows how to act properly at one of these things, anyway."

McGraw hung up on him.

TWENTY-THREE

Rhineheart walked into O'Brien's a few minutes after seven. Farnsworth was sitting on a stool at the bar. He was drinking a beer and talking Derby statistics with Sam. "Decidedly win the '62 Derby. Roman Line was second. Ridan run third."

"I thought Chateaugay won in '62."

Farnsworth shook his head. "Chateaugay was '63. Never Bend run second. Candy Spots was third."

"Who won it in '64?"

"Northern Dancer. Beat Hill Rise by a long neck. The Scoundrel got third."

"You know your shit."

Farnsworth nodded proudly.

Sam looked at Rhineheart. "The usual?"

Rhineheart nodded. "And give my friend here another beer."

"Your friend knows his shit," Sam said, and walked down to the end of the bar.

"You still follow the ponies?" Rhineheart asked Farnsworth. In the old days Farnsworth took two vacations a year. The spring meet and the fall meet.

Farnsworth nodded.

"You do any good?"

"You kidding? I'm lucky if I cash three tickets a year. Horses I bet to win run second, horses I bet to place show, horses I bet to show run out. But I ain't crying. You get used to losing. All I ask is that they don't ban me from the place. Let me sit out there with a couple of bucks in my pocket and a racing form waiting for the next race to come up." Farnsworth took a small sip of beer. "You go see Clark?"

Rhineheart nodded. "He offered me a job."

"You already got a job."

"That's what I told him."

"What kind of money did he talk?"

"Sixty-five thousand a year."

Farnsworth let out a whistle. "Jesus, what are they hiding, kid?"

"Good question. Another good question is who are 'they'?"

"It's a case full of good questions," said Farnsworth. "Beginning with who killed Walsh, and Sanchez, and the girl? And why?"

"You got any ideas?"

Farnsworth nodded. In his humble opinion, he said, there were a half a dozen suspects: Corrati; John Hughes; Howard Taggert; Duke Kingston; Walsh's wife; Gilmore. He wasn't ruling anybody out. All of them had motive and opportunity.

And it seemed to him that the question of who killed who was only a part of the puzzle. There was the syringe found in Walsh's bag in the airport locker. What was that all about? And now these missing foal papers. How did they fit in? For that matter, how did Sanchez fit in? Was he a friend of Walsh's? What about the money Walsh owed Marvin, who worked for Corrati? Did it have anything to do with Carl Walsh's disappearance and subsequent death? It looked as if everything was somehow tied in with Churchill Downs and the Derby. But maybe, Farnsworth said, that was because just about everyone involved in the case worked at the track.

"What do you think, Rhineheart?"

Rhineheart shrugged. Thinking about the case made him dizzy. "I think," he said, "that I'm going out to the airport and see this cabbie who picked up Walsh last Wednesday. What are you going to do?"

"If it's okay with you, I'm going to keep looking for

Walsh's wife. If she's not dead somewhere, she's on the run for some reason and scared. She may be the key to this thing. Also, I'm checking out a couple of other things. Nothing worth mentioning as yet."

"You always were a closemouthed old bastard, you know that?"

Farnsworth shrugged. "Loose lips sink ships."

"You need any money," Rhineheart said, "stop by the office and see McGraw. She'll take care of you."

"She the girlie who answers the phone for you?"

Rhineheart nodded. "She's good people."

"I used to have a dame answer the phone for me." Farnsworth's tone was wistful. "Back in the old days."

"This one doesn't want to answer the phone all her life. She'd like to be a private eye."

"No shit? You're kidding me."

"The world's changing, old man."

Farnsworth nodded glumly. "Yeah, I know."

At eight o'clock Rhineheart was standing in front of the Eastern Airlines exit at the airport when Independent cab 41, a green Dodge, pulled up to the curb. He walked over, opened the door, and got in the backseat. A black guy with sad droopy eyes turned around and said, "Where to, mister?"

"You J. T. Smith?"

"Who's asking?"

Rhineheart handed him a twenty.

The cabby smiled. "J. T. Smith, at your service."

"Last Wednesday night," Rhineheart said, "you picked up a fare at the Parkland Arms."

Smith nodded. "Blond-haired guy. Sharp features. Middle thirties."

"You remember where you took him?"

Smith nodded. "Sure do." He smiled.

Rhineheart took out another twenty.

"Took him over to Preston Street."

Preston Street? What the hell was on Preston street?

"Whereabouts on Preston Street?"

"The 2800-hundred block."

"A residence?"

J. T. Smith shook his head. "A shopping center. He had me drop him in the middle of this little shopping strip. Called the Midtown Shopping Village, something like that. I thought it was funny 'cause it was after nine and all the stores was closed."

"Did you see anyone waiting for him, anything like that?"

Smith shook his head. "Man just got out of the car and walked over toward some closed stores. I got another call about that time so I just took óff, you understan'."

Rhineheart handed him another twenty. "Thanks for the help."

"Don't mention it," Smith said. "Anytime."

Rhineheart started to get out of the cab.

Smith said, "Hey, mister, you a shamus, or something?"

Shamus. It was a word Farnsworth might have used.

"Yeah," Rhineheart said. "I'm a shamus, all right."

"I thought so," Smith said. "You act like one. You don't hardly see no private eyes around anymore. Not like you used to."

That's because we're disappearing, Rhineheart thought. Like dinosaurs. Pretty soon the species would be extinct. Maybe it already was. Maybe he and Farnsworth were the last of the breed. When Farnsworth was gone Rhineheart would be the last one.

The last private eye.

The Midtown Shopping Village consisted of a dozen retail stores, a health spa, a grocery, and a storefront real estate office. Rhineheart sat in the Maverick for twenty minutes, smoking and thinking and watching cars pull in and out of the parking lot. Then he got out and strolled over to the real estate office. The front door was locked and had a CLOSED sign on it. The window was lettered SOUTH END REAL ESTATE CORP. He pressed his face up to the glass, but there wasn't much to see. A desk with a typewriter and a telephone on it near the door. A couple of filing cabinets against the side wall. A carpeted floor. Another desk farther back. Behind that, a wall that faced the front window. A door in the wall. Who, he wondered, owned South End Real Estate? It looked as if tomorrow he was going to have to make another stop at the County Tax Assessor's office.

TWENTY-FOUR

Rhineheart ate dinner at a seafood restaurant near the river. He had Boston scrod and scallops and baby shrimp and hush puppies, washing it down with hot coffee.

Then he drove home.

He fixed a pot of Irish tea and watched part of an old movie on the television. When the movie was over, he switched off the TV and got into bed. He was almost asleep when the phone rang.

On the other end of the line a woman's voice, taut with fear, said, "This is Rhonda Walsh. Someone told me you want to talk to me."

"Where are you, Rhonda?"

"Never mind where I am. What do you want to talk to me about?"

"You know about Carl?"

"I read about it. The paper says it was an accident. It was no accident, it was murder."

"You know who did it?"

"You're damn right I know who did it. That bastard Corrati did it. He killed Carl because Carl owed him some money." She started to cry.

"Rhonda, you got any proof of what you're saying?"

"Proof? No, I don't have any *proof*. But everyone knows Corrati done it. He threatened Carl."

"Why don't you tell that to the cops?"

"You gotta be kidding. What are they going to do? Corrati pays off the police."

"Why don't you let me come and talk to you."

"Mister, I don't know who you are, or who you work for, or anything. My friend told me an old guy gave her this number."

"Listen, Rhonda, I'm working for somebody who wanted to find Carl before he got hurt."

"Sure you are, and I'm the tooth fairy. Listen, the reason I called is to tell you I'm leaving town. Put out the word. I'm gone and won't be back."

"Wait a minute, Rhonda."

"I may send you something belongs to Carl. My friend says the old guy's a nice guy."

"Rhonda."

The line went dead.

Rhinehcart went back to bed. He thought about the call for a while, then he started thinking about the last time he'd seen Jessica Kingston, replaying the encounter over in his mind. He told himself it was a waste of time to keep thinking about her. He put her out of his mind and after a while it was two in the morning and he was lying there staring at the ceiling and not thinking about her when the doorbell rang. He got up and got his gun, put on his robe, and went to the door.

Jessica Kingston was standing there.

The first thing she said was "What happened to your head?"

"I banged it against a blackjack."

The second thing she said was, "Are you all right?"

Rhineheart shrugged. "I'm okay."

The next thing she said was "You won't need that," and pointed at the gun.

Rhineheart put the gun down, slid his arm around her waist, pulled her to him, and kissed her. Her mouth came open immediately, her arms wrapping around his neck. She tasted and smelled of whiskey and cigarette smoke and expensive scent—and something else, something sweet and warm and full of promise, something distinctly her own. After a long moment they broke apart, both breathing audibly. Jessica Kingston's face looked stunned, as if she had just witnessed some momentous event, a five-car collision or something. Rhineheart knew how she felt. Even though he couldn't see his reflection, he was sure his own face had that same pale, shocked look.

Jessica Kingston said, "I don't even know your first name."

"It's Michael," Rhineheart said.

"Michael," she repeated.

He took her hand and led her into the bedroom.

"Let me help you undress."

She nodded. "Yes. Please."

Rhineheart woke in the middle of the night. The scent of sex mingled with the smell of cigarette smoke and perfume. She was stretched out on the bed next to him. The tip of her cigarette glowed in the dark. He reached over and touched her arm.

"You all right?"

"I'm fine. You?"

"I'm all right."

"I've been waiting for you to wake up," she said. "I want you to make love to me again." She stubbed out her cigarette in the ashtray on the night table. Then she turned to him. He reached over and cupped her breasts in his hands. Her nipples tightened. She shuddered with desire as he drew her to him. He entered her, thrusting deep, and her body rose to move against his in urgent yet easy rhythm.

"Oh God, yes."

"You like that?"

"Yes."

"And this?"

She moaned.

The sex was hot and fierce and sweet and what surprised Rhineheart most was the depth and force of the feelings evoked. It had been a long time since he had felt anything like the flood of emotions that went coursing through him. Not since Catherine. Maybe not ever. He wasn't sure how she felt, but at the end, as they clung together, limbs entwined, tears spilled out of her eyes and ran down her face. Afterward, they talked for an hour, then made love again, then slept, wrapped in each other's arms.

Later, Rhineheart woke to find her getting dressed. He looked at the clock on the dresser: 4:50.

"I have to go," she explained. "It's a long drive back to Lexington. I have a million things to do for tomorrow."

"Sure," Rhineheart said. The thing, as always, was to be cool.

"Help me with this, please."

He helped her with her dress.

"When will I see you again, Michael?"

"I'm coming to your party tomorrow."

"Tonight," she corrected him.

"Right."

"Yes, of course, but that's not what I mean. I want to see you again. Regularly. We'll have to make some arrangements. Find a place to meet. Someplace private."

"We can meet here," Rhineheart said.

"Yes, but we'll have to be careful."

He thought about that for a moment. Okay. He could live with that. He could handle it. If it meant seeing her, he could handle a lot of things.

"I have a private telephone that no one knows about. It rings in my bedroom." She gave him the number. "If you ever need me for anything, call me there."

"All right."

"I'm incredibly busy now, but after the Derby, things will calm down. We'll have more time," she said. "We'll be able to see each other as often as we want. We'll go places, if you like."

"I'll take you to the Vogue," Rhineheart said.

"Where?"

"It's a movie theater over on Lexington Road. They show a lot of old movies. You like old movies?"

"Yes."

"You like popcorn? I'll buy you some popcorn."

"How delightful."

She finished dressing. Rhineheart pulled on some slacks and a shirt and walked her outside to her car, a silver Porsche.

She put her hand up and touched his face.

"I'll see you at the party, Michael."

Rhineheart said, "We haven't talked about the case at all."

"No," she said. "We haven't had time, have we?"

"You know that Carl Walsh is dead?"

"I heard about it, yes." She shuddered. "Terrible."

"The police didn't find any foal papers in his car."

"Maybe he hid them someplace. Maybe he didn't take them after all." She looked at her watch. "I have to go, Michael."

"Be careful driving home," Rhineheart said.

They kissed good-bye and she got in her car and Rhineheart watched her drive off. He stood in the street, staring after her car a long time after the taillights had disappeared.

TWENTY-FIVE

Rhineheart didn't go back to bed. He drove over to Bellarmine and ran for half an hour. When he got back home he removed his bandages, took a shower, and got dressed. He ate breakfast at a donut shop on Taylorsville Road and read the paper. They carried a brief account of Walsh's death. It was on page six of the second section.

The sports section had an article about the draw for post position for the Derby. The ceremony was being held at the racing secretary's office at 10:00 A.M. It was 9:40. If he drove like hell he could make it about the time it was over. The hell with it.

After breakfast, he drove downtown to the County Clerk's office. He parked in an OFFICIALS ONLY spot and took the stairs to the Tax Assessor's office. He had a different clerk pull the file on South End Real Estate Corp. The president of South End was Curtis Evans of Louisville, a name he didn't recognize. On the form, the company was described as a subsidiary of Midtown Properties. He asked the clerk to pull the Midtown Properties file.

And struck pay dirt. Such as it was.

The owner and chief presiding officer of Midtown Properties was none other than Harrison Gilmore. That meant what? He could tie the vet to the company that owned a store in a place that Carl Walsh had taken a cab to on the night he disappeared. Big deal. He thanked the clerk, went back out to the Maverick, and drove over to police headquarters.

Katz's office was a little partition with a desk on the third floor. He was typing up a report when Rhineheart arrived. He opened a desk drawer, reached inside, took out a small manila envelope, ripped it open, and dumped a brown leather wallet on the top of the desk. He jerked his thumb at it. "Walsh's."

Rhineheart looked through the wallet. Driver's license. Social security card. Employee Pass. Visa Card. A Gulf Oil credit card. A wad of business cards in the billfold. On the back of one card was a phone number. Rhineheart memorized it, put the card back into the wallet, the wallet back into the manila envelope.

"Find anything, peeper?"

He shook his head.

Katz scowled at him. "Guess what?"

"Huh?"

"Walsh's wife hasn't showed up to claim the body yet."

"No kidding?"

"You wouldn't happen to know why she hasn't showed up, would you?"

"Maybe she's busy, Katz."

"Get out of here."

Rhineheart decided to spend the rest of the morning tailing Gilmore. A call to the vet's office elicited the information that on Thursdays Gilmore didn't come in until the afternoon. Rhineheart drove over to Gilmore's house, a large, elegant Victorian home near Cherokee Park, and parked down the block. He had with him a container of coffee and a couple of glazed donuts in case he got hungry, and a paperback collection of short stories in the event he got bored.

He sat there sipping coffee and smoking and waiting for Gilmore to make an appearance. At 12:30 Gilmore came out of the house and got into a silver-gray Cadillac, which was parked in the driveway. He pulled out of the driveway and turned left. Rhineheart waited until the Cadillac reached the end of the block before he wheeled the Maverick out into the street and followed.

Gilmore took Bardstown Road to the Watterson Expressway, the expressway east to Shelbyville Road. His office was in a three-story brick-and-glass office building across the street from a shopping center.

Gilmore pulled the Cadillac into the office building parking lot, whipped into a reserved parking space, got out, and entered the building. Rhineheart parked across the street in the shopping center. He turned on the radio, twisting the dial around until he found a news show. He listened to the news for a few minutes. It was the same old shit. Then he turned the radio off. He read part of a short story, smoked four cigarettes. Stakeouts were another pain in the ass. You needed to be patient, cool. Rhineheart wasn't that patient.

After a while he grew restless and decided to nose around and see what he could see. He got out of the Maverick, walked across the street and took the elevator up to the third floor. Gilmore's office was at the end of the hall. As he stepped off the elevator, the door to the office opened and Gilmore came out and walked toward Rhineheart. He was wearing a checkered sports coat, yellow slacks, and white shoes with a gold buckle across the instep. Gilmore had his head down and he was carrying a small black leather bag, similar to a doctor's bag.

Before Gilmore could look up, Rhineheart opened the door on his immediate right and stepped inside. The men's john. Cold tile. Chrome faucets. Urinals. Stalls. Bright, gleaming mirrors. Rhineheart went ahead and relieved himself. It had been a long wait in the car. He washed his hands and dried them, staring at his reflection in the mirror. He waited an extra thirty seconds, then opened the door. No one was in the hall. The elevator floor indicator was moving down past 2 toward 1.

Rhineheart took the stairs down and made it to the building entrance at the same time Gilmore was climbing into the Cadillac. He waited for the Cadillac to pull out of the lot and turn right before he ran across the street to the Maverick, got in, hit the starter, and headed after it.

He caught up to the Cadillac as it was turning up the westbound ramp of the Watterson Expressway. Rhineheart eased up on the gas, trying to keep a couple of cars and fifty yards between the Maverick and the Cadillac.

They traveled west for five minutes, then the Cadillac's

turning signal flashed on and it swung up the Newburg Road exit, headed north. Gilmore continued on Newburg for another mile, then, at Trevillian Way, he turned left.

He drove past the Collings' estate and the tennis center and turned into the parking lot of the Louisville Zoo. The zoo? What the hell. Rhineheart flipped on his left turn signal, waiting for a couple of cars to pass, and watched Gilmore pull into an empty parking space near the front of the lot. Then he turned in, parked the Maverick farther back, and got his binoculars out of the glove compartment.

In a few minutes a Green Turino drove into the lot and parked a few spaces away from the Cadillac. A man got out of the car, carrying a small plastic case. Rhineheart put the binoculars on him. A tall thin man with red hair and freckles. It was the guy he had seen sitting at Corrati's table in the Kitty Kat Club on Saturday night.

The redheaded guy walked over and got into the front seat of the Cadillac. He and Gilmore talked for ten minutes, then the redheaded guy got out of the car—no longer carrying the case. He got into the Turino and drove toward the exit. Rhineheart decided to drop Gilmore and follow the redheaded guy.

The Turino traveled down Trevillian to Poplar Level, south on Poplar Level to the Watterson west exit. On the expressway, the redheaded guy drove like a madman, whipping in and out of traffic, changing lanes. Rhineheart had to floor the Maverick to keep up.

Ten minutes later he watched the Turino swing down the Camp Ground Road exit and turn left. The redheaded guy seemed to be headed for Rubbertown, a section of the city that was populated with industrial chemical plants. The Turino cruised past the Dupont plant and turned left on Bell's Lane, then left again onto a small two-lane road that curved in the direction of the river. There was little traffic on the road. It was easy to be spotted. Rhineheart slowed down.

A few miles farther on, the Turino turned into a parking lot adjoining a squat yellow-brick building. The lettered sign that ran across the face of the building read WESTERN CHEMICALS.

Rhineheart pulled over to the side of the road and shut

off the engine. He watched the redheaded man get out of the Turino and walk in the building.

He started up the car and pulled into the chemical company parking lot. He went in the same entrance that the redheaded guy had used. Just inside the door, a receptionist sat behind a desk. A nameplate that read MS. MARSHALL sat next to the telephone on her desk.

Rhineheart waved an old deputy sheriff's badge in front of her. "Detective Sergeant Katz," he said. "Traffic enforcement. The gentleman who just came in here . . . ?"

"Mr. Lewis?" the receptionist said.

LEWIS W. C.: Lewis. Western Chemicals.

Rhineheart nodded. "Lewis, that's right. He's a . . . your . . . ?"

"Chief chemist."

"Chief chemist. That's right."

"Is anything the matter? Do you want to see Mr. Lewis?"

"*Who?*"

"Mr. Lewis, the man you just asked about."

"Lewis? I thought the man I was following was named Stewart."

"Sir, are you referring to the redheaded man who just entered this building?"

"The man I was after had black hair."

"I'm afraid Mr. Lewis has red hair."

"Obviously, this is a case of mistaken identity," Rhineheart said. "I'm probably in the wrong building, too."

The receptionist looked thoroughly confused.

On his way out Rhineheart told her to have a nice day.

TWENTY-SIX

Rhineheart drove downtown to the office. McGraw was hunched over the typewriter, either working on a new letter, or retyping the one she had screwed up on Monday.

Rhineheart noticed something green and leafy on his desk.

"What's this shit?"

"A plant. I thought the place could use a little color."

"This is a detective agency," Rhineheart said, "not a greenhouse."

"One little plant isn't going to hurt anything."

"Just keep it over on *your* desk, okay?"

"Okay." McGraw cleared her throat nervously. "I bought something else. I went shopping this morning and got a new dress."

"That's nice."

"For the party tonight," she said.

"Fine."

"I put it on the office expense account."

"How much?" Rhineheart said.

"You're going to kill me."

"How much?"

"It really wasn't that expensive," she said.

"Why am I going to kill you, then?"

"You just are."

"Give me a figure, McGraw."

"Promise not to yell."

Rhineheart shook his head. "No promises."

"It was $125.95."

"That sounds about right," Rhineheart said.

"You're not upset?" She looked disappointed. "I should've got the purse and shoes that went with it."

"Farnsworth call?" Rhineheart asked.

McGraw shook her head. "Was he supposed to?"

Rhineheart nodded. It had been eighteen hours since he had heard from Farnsworth. Usually, the old man was pretty good about keeping in touch.

"You worried about him?"

"Naw," he lied.

"Can I go home now? It's gonna take me about five hours to get ready for the party."

"I'll pick you up in an hour and a half."

After she left, Rhineheart called Johnny Reardon of Midtown Investigations. He was an old friend, an ex-associate.

"It's Rhineheart, John."

"How's himself these days?" Reardon asked in his fake Irish brogue.

"Himself's doing okay. How about you, buddy?"

"Fine as wine. What can I do for you?"

"I need you to run a background on somebody," Rhineheart said. Background meant the whole bit: home and work address, phone number, employment record, next of kin, credit check, police record, bank accounts, tax data, medical history, military record. Whatever information you could get. Reardon was an ace at running backgrounds. He knew all the people who knew all the stuff.

"I got a name," Rhineheart said, "and a place of employment."

"More than enough, me boyo."

Rhineheart gave him Lewis's name and the name and address of the chemical company.

"Cost you the usual bill. Have it ready for you Saturday."

"One more thing, John. I want you to check out Thoroughbred Security, a Lexington firm. Find out who owns it, who sits on the board, etc."

"You got it."

Rhineheart hung up and called Farnsworth's office. He

wasn't in, and his answering service didn't know how to reach him.

Rhineheart decided to try the number he had found in Walsh's wallet.

The phone rang once. It was picked up and a familiar voice said, "Howard Taggert here."

Rhineheart was surprised, but he didn't let on. "Taggert. This is Michael Rhineheart, the private detective who came to see you the other day."

"How'd you get this number? It's private and unlisted."

"Carl Walsh gave it to me."

Taggert snorted. "That's highly unlikely."

"The truth is, I found this number in Carl Walsh's wallet, and I didn't mention it to the police."

Taggert was silent for a moment. "What is it you want?"

"For one thing, I want to know what he was doing with your private unlisted number in his wallet."

"You have no authority or right to ask me any questions."

"You want the cops to ask you about it? They've got enough authority."

There was another silence. Then Taggert said, "Last Tuesday morning Walsh came up to me as I was leaving the track kitchen. He said he had something I might be interested in, a tape recording that showed evidence of some illegal activity on the part of certain horsemen who were stabled at the Downs. He wouldn't name names. Walsh offered to sell this material to me. I told him that if he really had such evidence, he was obligated to take it to the stewards, but he said he would throw it away before he would give it away. He wanted someone to buy the information from him. He hinted that the illegal activity concerned the Derby. He said he would sell the tape recording to the first person who would give him enough money. To forestall this, I gave Walsh my number and told him to call me that same evening. He never did."

"You were going to buy the evidence from him?"

"If necessary, yes."

"Then what were you going to do with it?"

"Turn it over to the stewards, of course."

Of course.

"Walsh didn't tell you *anything* about the evidence? What it concerned? Who it was about?"

"No."

Why would Walsh go to Taggert? There were only two logical reasons: either he had something on Taggert and wanted to blackmail him; or the evidence was on Kingston and he knew Taggert would be interested in it.

"Tell me something," Rhineheart said. "Why do you think Walsh came to *you?*"

"I don't really know. Maybe because he worked for me once. Maybe because he knew I was a member of the board of directors at the Downs."

"Did Walsh hint that Kingston might be involved?"

"As I said, Walsh didn't mention any names."

"You go to the stewards about your encounter with Walsh?"

"And tell them what? My version of Walsh's vague accusations against nameless people? Not hardly, sir."

"Are you still interested in the recording?"

"Why? Do you have it? Is that the reason you called me?"

"You still willing to pay money for it?"

"That depends on what you're asking for it."

Taggert was a real cutie. Rhineheart said, "You better get yourself a lawyer, Jack. If it turns out Walsh was murdered, the police are going to want to talk to you about withholding evidence."

"Murdered?"

"Yeah," Rhineheart said, "and one more thing. If I come across this recording, you're the last fucking person I'd send it to."

He slammed down the phone on the old bastard and went home to change for the party.

TWENTY-SEVEN

Rhineheart picked up McGraw in front of her apartment. She was pacing the sidewalk nervously. The hundred-and-twenty-five-dollar dress was black and simple and knee length. A strand of pearls encircled her neck and she clutched a glittery black evening bag.

She slid into the passenger seat. "How do I look? Be honest."

"You clean up pretty good," Rhineheart told her. "What about me?" He was wearing a rented Lord West outfit.

"What *about* you?"

"How do *I* look?"

McGraw shrugged. "You look like you always look. A big guy in a wrinkled suit. Only this time it's a wrinkled tux."

"Thanks." Rhineheart eased away from the curb. He took a look at his watch. It was 7:35. The next time he checked it, it was 8:49, and the Maverick was rolling up to the twin pillars in front of Cresthill.

The entrance was guarded by a half dozen blue-uniformed guards who wore side arms. The patches on their shoulders read THOROUGHBRED SECURITY. They looked Rhineheart's invitation over closely, but finally waved him through.

The party looked to be in full swing, the huge striped tent was ablaze with lights. The blacktop farm road was lined on both sides with big expensive cars.

"God damn," McGraw said, looking around in awe.

Rhineheart nodded. "It's something, isn't it?"

He pulled up near the front entrance to the tent. A parking attendant wearing jockey's silks opened the door for McGraw, then ran around and opened his door. The attendant wrote the license number on a ticket, handed it to Rhineheart, hopped into the Maverick, and peeled off.

McGraw pointed up the hill. "Is that the house?" The huge mansion was outlined against the night sky, its tall white columns lit by floodlights.

"That's it."

"Jesus."

As they strolled up to the tent entrance, Rhineheart made the mistake of saying, "When we get inside, try to be cool, okay?"

McGraw looked offended. "What do you mean, 'try to be cool'? I'm always cool."

"All I'm saying," Rhineheart said, "is watch how you talk inside. You swear a lot, McGraw."

"*I* swear a lot?"

"Yeah, and these people might not go for that."

They entered the tent and came abreast of another couple, middle-aged, dressed to the teeth.

In a loud voice, McGraw said, "Rhineheart, you think I'm going to go around and call everybody a motherfucker, or something?"

The couple's heads swiveled in unison. Rhineheart grabbed McGraw's arm and steered her over to an unoccupied table, covered with a white linen tablecloth. At the surrounding tables, the men were all tanned and healthy-looking, the women glamorous and bejeweled. He and McGraw were encircled by the rich and the powerful. In evening wear and glitzy gowns, the rich and powerful looked rather formidable.

Rhineheart looked around the tent. Brightly colored balloons hung from the ceiling. The tent poles were festooned with intricately tied crepe paper. There were half a dozen large buffet tables filled with food. And half a dozen bars stocked with bottles of the finest booze and wines. *Sumptuous* was the word.

There was a dance floor in the center of the tent and a twelve-piece band was playing. Twelve middle-aged white guys. They sounded, to Rhineheart, like Lester Lanin. The dance floor was crowded.

"Your kind of music," he told McGraw. "Want to dance?"

McGraw shook her head. "I'm too nervous."

Waitresses wearing jockey's caps and short fluffy skirts scurried in and out among the tables. Rhineheart ordered bourbon and water. McGraw asked for a mint julep.

"No beer?"

McGraw shook her head. "Nothing but classy drinks tonight." She smiled at Rhineheart. "I'm surprised you and the waitress aren't old friends."

"Actually," Rhineheart said, "she looks familiar."

McGraw was gazing past his shoulder. "Somebody's heading our way. He looks important."

Rhineheart turned around. Duke Kingston was making his way toward their table. "It's our host," Rhineheart told McGraw.

"Isn't he a handsome devil."

Kingston came up to the table. He didn't offer to shake hands, but he was friendly enough. "Mr. Rhineheart, good to see you." He turned to McGraw. "Who's this lovely lady?"

Rhineheart did the honors. "Sally McGraw ... Duke Kingston."

"It's a great pleasure to meet you, ma'am. Are you enjoying the party?"

"It's very nice," McGraw said.

"Supah. Supah." Kingston turned back to Rhineheart. "Understand the police found Walsh's body in the river. Said he was drunk. Said it was an accident." He paused. "What do you think, Mr. Rhineheart?"

Rhineheart shrugged. "What do I know?"

Kingston smiled. "You not a big talker, are you? Well," he added, "why should you be, huh?" He looked around the room, beaming.

The equivalent of a flashbulb went off inside Rhineheart's head. "Tell me something," he said to Kingston.

"Sho."

"Who's your vet?"

"I beg your pardon?"

"The veterinarian for Cresthill Farms. Who is it?"

"Dr. Harrison Gilmore. Why do you ask?"

"No reason," Rhineheart said. It was a question he should have asked someone days ago. He hadn't been thinking. He should have known that most vets worked for more than one farm.

Kingston took his arm. "It's too bad about the ten thousand dollars, but look here, Mr. Rhineheart, you enjoy yourself tonight. Feel free to mingle about and party to your heart's content. I don't want you or your lady-friend to feel like you're out of your element one bit. We're all just folks around here." He patted Rhineheart on the shoulder and strode off.

Rhineheart looked at McGraw. "He doesn't want us to feel out of our element."

"He's a real prince," McGraw said. She took a hit of her julep. "I'm gonna mingle about and party some. You want to come?"

"You go ahead," Rhineheart said. "But keep your eye on Kingston. If he leaves the party, let me know."

McGraw drifted away. Rhineheart sat there staring down into his drink, as if there were a message in there, among the rocks of ice and the oily dregs of booze. A notion was starting to take shape in his brain. It had nothing to do with logic or deduction, it was nothing clear and sharp and definite. It was more like a pattern emerging against a background of facts. His mind was running through connections, links between a veterinarian, a chemist, a gambler, a couple of stable hands who worked for different stables, Derby horses, and owners. In this context it seemed that the most important question was not necessarily *who* had killed Carl Walsh, but *why* had he been killed? Maybe he'd known something. And maybe that something concerned one of the horses in the Derby. Rhineheart sat there, rapt in thought, oblivious to the scene around him.

A hand touched his arm.

"Michael."

He looked up, and Jessica Kingston was standing there. He looked at her face and realized that in some corner of his mind he had been thinking about her all day, and his throat filled up and his chest began to hurt. She was no one-night lady and she was lovely beyond all saying. She was wearing a full-length dress. Her arms and shoulders were bare. Her hair was pulled back from her face in a knot. Her eyes were clear, her gaze was serene.

"Hi," he said.

"You look so lonely sitting here, Michael. Are you all right?"

"Sure."

"Are you enjoying yourself?"

"It's a nice party."

"Thank you. I was hoping you'd be here. Hoping I'd see you."

"What about you?" Rhineheart said. "Are you okay?"

"I'm fine. Would you like me to introduce you to the duchess?"

"Who?"

"The guest of honor, the Duchess of Sussex."

"Naw, I don't think so." He stood up. "What about a dance?"

She smiled. "Yes, that would be nice."

Rhineheart took her hand and led her out onto the floor. Half a dozen couples were dancing. He took Jessica in his arms and they began to dance slowly in a small space on the floor. She fit into his arms perfectly. The band was playing some romantic ballad in the blandest way imaginable. They were playing it all wrong, but it didn't matter to Rhineheart. All that counted was that her head came to rest against his chest and they were in each other's arms and moving together in rhythm to the music.

She whispered something he couldn't quite understand. He asked her to repeat it, but she just shook her head and smiled.

When the song ended, she looked at him and said, "Thank you for asking me, Michael. It was nice."

"It was my pleasure."

"I have to get back to my guests."

"I understand."

She disappeared into a crowd of people. Rhineheart looked around. McGraw was standing there on the edge of the floor. He walked over and borrowed a cigarette from her.

"You better watch yourself," McGraw said. "You've got it bad."

"You think so, huh?"

"I know so. And so does everyone else who saw you two on the floor." She shook her head. "Rhineheart, it's an awful big jump from waitresses to socialites."

"I'll keep that in mind," Rhineheart said. He looked around the room. "Where's Kingston?"

"He left about five minutes ago," McGraw said. "You were dancing. I followed him outside. He got in a car and drove up to the mansion."

"I'm going to take a little stroll," Rhineheart said. "Hang around here and see what you can see."

"Be careful."

As he was walking away, an overdressed matronly lady seized McGraw by the arm.

"Oh God," she said. "I love your gown. Is it a Halston?"

McGraw nodded. "As a matter of fact, it is."

"Who are you?" the woman said. "Are you famous?"

"Yes."

"Oh God, I knew it. Are you an actress? Movies or TV?"

"TV."

Rhineheart wandered slowly over to an exit, checked to see if anyone was watching him, then stepped outside and headed across the grounds toward the mansion. It was a cloudy cool night. The grass was wet with dew. He made a wide circle through a grove of trees, stopping every now and then to see if he was being followed. He had the sense that someone was behind him, but he couldn't spot anyone. It was probably nerves. He came out of the trees on the far side of the house.

He was fifty feet from the house, and across the garden,

through the windows of the French doors, he could see a group of figures inside the house—seated in the library. Keeping low to the ground, he moved slowly across the garden.

He edged up to the windows and looked inside.

TWENTY-EIGHT

Six men were seated around the large conference table near the fireplace. They were grouped around the far end of the table. On one side—Duke Kingston, Angelo Corrati, and Gilmore. On the other—Hughes, the redheaded chemist Lewis, and Calvin Clark. Clark was the only real surprise. Not a big one, but still a surprise.

The others, yeah, he had stirred their names into the pot that had been stewing in his head for the past couple of days. But he had not considered Clark. He'd felt, he guessed, that Clark was too powerful, too important, and above all too slick to let himself get involved in something as crude and ordinary as a stable hand's murder. Clark's presence indicated that it was something more than that.

From where he stood he could see everyone clearly, but their voices were indistinct, muffled by the thick glass of the French doors.

Corrati was speaking. On the table in front of him sat an open briefcase. It was full of stacks of hundred-dollar bills.

Rhineheart had to strain to hear, but he caught some of the words and phrases: "track odds . . . seven to one . . . a sixteen-dollar bill . . . two hundred thousand times . . . 2.8 million . . . stopover in . . . arrive four, four-thirty . . . Vegas . . ."

Kingston stood up and said something to the effect that although Corrati had joined their little group late and through the back door so to speak, he was nevertheless, "a valuable addition, a man from whom we can all learn something." Then Kingston said something to Lewis, who stood up, his back to the windows, and began to speak in a low voice. The only words Rhineheart could make out were *dosage* and *untraceability*.

He was going to have to get closer. There was a window opposite the far end of the table. It was next to the fireplace on the west side of the house. He backed away from the French doors, moved to his right through some flower beds, and found a path that led alongside the house. He followed it until the window was ten feet ahead and on his left. He was heading for it when a man stepped out from behind a hedge, pointed a gun at him, and said, "Freeze."

Rhineheart froze. The moon was a bright yellow ball that hung in the sky above the treetops. By its light, he could see that the man with the gun was wearing the same dark blue police-style uniform as the men at the farm entrance. A tag above the pocket said WILSON.

"Put your hands up," the man told Rhineheart.

Rhineheart put his hands up.

The guard gestured with the gun. "Turn around."

Rhineheart did as he was told; then something cold and hard slammed against the back of his head. He felt himself falling forward and blacking out.

When he opened his eyes he was lying facedown in a flower bed. Voices drifted down to him.

Kingston: "Take him down to the old stallion barn. We're getting ready to tear it down. It's off by itself and deserted. We'll have to finish him there."

Clark: "Duke! There are three people already dead. This thing is getting out of hand."

Kingston: "What choice do we have, Calvin? Tell me that."

There was no reply.

Tell him a choice, Calvin, Rhineheart wanted to say. Think up something.

Kingston: "We'll make it look like an accident. Get Doc to give him an injection of something."

Rhineheart tried to raise his head. A voice he didn't recognize said, "He's starting to wake up."

"Hit him again," Kingston said. "Harder this time."

The blow wasn't any harder than the first one, but it was

enough to put him under: the world faded out. When it faded back in, he was sitting in a circle of light on the dirt floor of a barn, his back against a horse stall.

Duke Kingston, Clark, Gilmore, and Kingston's goon Borchek were standing a few feet away, staring down at him. Borchek was holding the Python, pointing it at Rhineheart, whose hands were bound behind his back with baling wire. His feet were untied. Free, in a manner of speaking. Maybe, he thought, I can tap-dance my way out of here.

He squinted up at the source of the light, a naked bulb that dangled from a chain attached to a roof beam. The bulb cast a harsh half-circle of light that extended out for twenty feet or so. Then it ended and the rest of the barn was dark.

For a moment Rhineheart thought he saw something, a figure, a shape, move in the darkness behind the light. Then he decided it was his imagination, or plain old fear, or both. The boogie man coming to get him.

He looked over at Clark. "What does this do to the job offer?"

Kingston showed Rhineheart his teeth. "Still joking, eh? Well, you goin' to need that sense of humor, Mr. Rhineheart. Considering what we got planned for you."

Borchek glowered. "You want me to shut him up, Mr. Kingston?"

Kingston shook his head. "Just watch him, Borchek. If I want anything done, I'll let you know."

"I just thought—"

Kingston silenced him with a look.

"It's what you get for hiring retards," Rhineheart said.

"Keep on with the jokes, Mr. Rhineheart. Your time is running out."

"How about answering a few questions before it does?"

Kingston shook his head. "Sorry."

"Come on. You're the ace when it comes to press conferences, Kingston. Just confirm a couple of things for me. Lewis discovered some kind of untraceable super drug. Brought it to you and Gilmore. You tested it on Royal Dancer in Florida. It worked. You tested it again in Arkansas by not giving it to Royal Dancer. And he lost. You tested it again on Lancelot. And somewhere along in there, Carl Walsh found out about your plot. So you killed him. And his friend Sanchez. And his girl friend. And you would have killed his wife if you could have found her. How am I doing so far?"

"Not bad, Mr. Rhineheart. But like I say, you're about to run out of time."

"How did Corrati get involved? Did Walsh go to him thinking Corrati'd help him blackmail you all? Didn't he know that Corrati wouldn't want any partners? I guess what I'm asking is who killed Walsh? You guys or Corrati?"

"Does it really make any difference, Mr. Rhineheart?"

"Let's get this over with," Clark said nervously.

Kingston turned to Gilmore. "Harrison?"

Gilmore dropped to one knee and opened the top of his medical bag. He withdrew a long, wicked-looking syringe from the bag. It was filled with a milky fluid.

"This ought to do the job," he said.

Rhineheart wasn't sure he wanted to know, but he asked anyway. "What is it?"

"It's sodium potassinate," Gilmore said in a flat, even voice.

"I think I'm allergic to it," Rhineheart said.

No one laughed.

"Plus," he said, "I'm not big on needles either."

Gilmore stood up, holding the needle upright in the manner of a medical professional, and walked toward him.

Rhineheart didn't have a plan. Every private eye was supposed to have a plan for moments like this one, but he couldn't think of one. His mind was blank.

Gilmore moved closer.

The way Rhineheart saw it, he could do one of two things: he could start crying and sniveling and beg Gilmore not to kill him, or he could kick the good doctor in the balls.

Rhineheart decided to kick him in the balls. As far as plans go, it wasn't hitting on much. It didn't address the question of what to do with Kingston, Clark, or Borchek, who was bigger than Too Tall Jones and had a gun to boot.

But it was something to do. Which, Rhineheart said to

himself, is always better than nothing. Maybe.

He drew his feet back as Gilmore came near, and at that moment, a familiar voice came booming out of the darkness:

"Faaareeeze!"

Gilmore froze. So did Borchek and Clark. Kingston spun around and faced Farnsworth, the old pro, whose shadowy outline could be seen in the darkness, poised in the classic two-handed firing stance, his weapon trained in their direction. Farnsworth had been his plan. All along. Rhineheart hadn't known it, but the old bastard had been following him around all day, backing him up.

"You okay, kid?"

"I'm okay, old man."

Farnsworth spoke to Kingston. "Tell the big jamoke to drop the gun. Tell the horse doctor to throw away the needle. And tell both of them to do it quick, or I'll blow a hole through all of your asses."

Kingston said, "You heard the man."

The Colt made a loud thump on the hay-strewn ground. Gilmore tossed the syringe toward the wall.

"Untie my associate, horse doctor, and be quick about it."

It took Gilmore several minutes to untie Rhineheart, whose hands had gone numb from the tightness of the bonds. He rubbed them together as he went over and picked up his weapon.

Farnsworth said, "Check and make sure that baby's loaded, Rhineheart."

Rhineheart spun the chamber. The weapon was loaded. "It's full," he told Farnsworth.

"Whhheeeewwwww." Farnsworth let out his breath in a long sigh, and stepped forward into the light. He was smiling and there was a look of relief on his long thin face. He held up his hand to show Rhineheart his weapon. It was a thick twig. "I ain't carried a gun since 1957," he said and cackled.

TWENTY-NINE

"What are we gonna do with them?" Farnsworth asked Rhineheart.

It was a good question. Were they going to take them in? If so, where was "in"? Cresthill Farms was in Fayette County. Who had jurisdiction here? The state cops or the Fayette County Sheriff's Office? How would either group react when a couple of gumshoes from a different part of the state walked in with one of the commonwealth's leading citizens and an incredible story about a plot to fix the Derby? Rhineheart didn't know for sure, but he had an idea.

"I don't know," he said to Farnsworth. "Maybe we ought to kill them."

Duke Kingston shook his head. "I don't think so. I don't think you're built that way, Mr. Rhineheart."

"No?" Rhineheart squeezed off a shot that whistled past Kingston's right ear. Kingston turned pale, but didn't flinch. He even managed a tight smile. "Maybe I was wrong," he said.

But he wasn't. Rhineheart couldn't kill the son of a bitch. Not cold like that. He gestured at the other three with the weapon. "Lie down. Next to each other. On your stomachs."

After some scrambling around, they did so. Rhineheart leaned over and gave each of them a little tap with the butt of the gun just below the occipital bone. It took them out.

He had to tap Borchek, who had a head like a cement block, twice.

"Wonder it didn't dent the gun butt" was Farnsworth's comment.

Rhineheart waved the gun at Kingston. "Move. You're going to be our way out of here."

A white pickup truck stood idling on the road outside the barn. Its lights were out. The words CRESTHILL FARMS were painted on the door.

"Looky here," Farnsworth said. "Isn't that thoughtful?"

Farnsworth climbed in behind the wheel. Rhineheart opened the passenger door, motioned Kingston in, then slid in next to him and closed the door. He pointed the barrel of the gun at Kingston's stomach.

"Tell us how to get back to the party."

Kingston pointed straight ahead. "Just follow the road."

Farnsworth punched on the headlights and shoved the truck into gear. The road wound through the stable area, past a cluster of barns.

"Left here. Then left again."

They turned onto the main farm road. Ahead, maybe half a mile, Rhineheart could see the glow of lights from the party tent.

"You're a lucky man, Mr. Rhineheart," Kingston broke the silence. "The question becomes . . . are you a reasonable one?"

"You're not going to make me another offer, are you?"

"Of course I am."

"Go ahead," Rhineheart said. "I'm listening."

"Drive straight home and go to bed and forget everything you overheard tonight. In exchange, I'll make you a rich man. And I'm not talking about any piddly-ass $65,000-a-year job offer now. I'm talking about more money than you ever seen in your whole life, more money than you ever dreamed of. Never mind the Derby winnin's. Do you have any conception of the kind of money that this drug Hughes discovered can make for us? I'm talking, my friend, about millions and millions of dollars, and the Derby is just the beginning, just the tip of the iceberg, so to speak."

Farnsworth shook his head. "You goddamn rich folk," he said. "Ain't you got enough?"

Kingston snickered. "Shit," he said, his voice dripping with contempt. "There's never *enough,* old-timer. Only a man without anything would talk that kind of crap."

The truck crept slowly along the road, which was lined on both sides with parked cars.

Rhineheart said, "Tell me something, Kingston. Where does your wife fit into this scheme?"

"Let's leave Jessica out of the discussion, Mr. Rhineheart. She keeps her nose out of my business, and I stay out of her affairs. If you know what I mean." He gave Rhineheart a cool challenging look.

Rhineheart made no reply. They were fifty yards from the tent.

Kingston said, "It'd be a mistake to go to the police, you know."

"You think so, huh?"

"You don't have any real evidence. Just your word that some events occurred. And from what I understand, your word is not highly thought of at police headquarters. On the other hand, I have some friends rather high up on the force. I can make a lot of trouble for you, Mr. Rhineheart."

"There's three people been killed," Farnsworth said. "That oughta cause a stink."

"I doubt it," Kingston said. "Three nobodies. Two hotwalkers and a barmaid."

"Bend over," Rhineheart told Kingston. He was tired of listening to the bastard and pissed off to boot.

"What?"

Rhineheart pushed Kingston's head forward and clipped him with the barrel of the gun. It wasn't the occipital bone, but it got the job done. Kingston groaned and slumped down in the seat.

"Here's the car," Farnsworth said, and whipped the pickup into a spot next to the Maverick. They got out. Kingston lay stretched out on the seat. It looked as if he'd be out for a while.

Farnsworth reached inside the pickup, took the keys out of the ignition, and flipped them over into the grass.

"You bring a car?" Rhineheart asked Farnsworth, who shook his head.

"I hitched a ride with a fella."

"How'd you get on the grounds?"

Farnsworth grinned and pulled open his suit coat. Underneath it, he was wearing a jockey's silk. "I'm supposed to be one of the car parkers."

Rhineheart tossed him the keys to the Maverick. "Bring it around to the tent entrance and wait for us." He jammed the gun down into his waistband, sprinted over to the tent, and went inside.

McGraw was standing near the dance floor, looking worried.

"You've been gone an hour and a half," she said angrily, then looked at his head and said, "You're bleeding."

"We've got to get out of here," Rhineheart said, looking around. The party was going full blast. The tent was wall-to-wall people. "Have you seen Jessica Kingston?"

McGraw nodded. "I talked to her. She came up and introduced herself to me. She knew I was with you. She gave me a message for you." McGraw handed him a folded piece of paper.

Dear Michael,

Took my houseguest into Lexington to see the sights—such as they are. Will talk to you tomorrow.

Love, .
Jessica

"Goddammit," Rhineheart said, "she's with the goddamn Duchess of somewhere."

"*Who?*"

Two men, one bald-headed, the other wearing a thick black beard, walked into the tent. They were wearing blazers with a logo over the breast pocket. The logo, Rhineheart knew, read THOROUGHBRED SECURITY.

He took McGraw's arm. "It's time to split." They walked outside. The Maverick was there, its engine chugging away. Farnsworth sat behind the wheel, gunning the motor. McGraw jumped in back, Rhineheart took the front passenger seat, and Farnsworth put it in gear. They took off down the farm road. At the main entrance the security guards waved them through. As far as Rhineheart could tell, no one followed them.

They spent the drive home discussing what Rhineheart had overhead and seen through the library window.

"Jesus Christ," McGraw said. "A plot to fix the Kentucky Derby."

Farnsworth said, "It's hard to believe, isn't it?"

"It's incredible."

"It's goddamn un-American is what it is."

It was one in the morning when they reached the Louisville city limits. They drove over to Rhineheart's place. He gave McGraw the bedroom, Farnsworth the couch, and he sat in the chair by the front window with his weapon ready, watching the street outside.

At 3:06 the phone rang. It was Kingston.

"You been waiting for my call, Mr. Rhineheart?"

"I wasn't sure it was going to be a call."

"You had a lucky night, Mr. Rhineheart. But I have a warning for you. Don't press this matter any further. Or someone innocent might get hurt."

Rhineheart's stomach suddenly felt hollow.

"What are you talking about, Kingston?"

"You know damn well what I'm talkin' about, Mr. Rhineheart. I'm talking about Jessica. You wouldn't want to see her get hurt, would you?"

"You wouldn't do that," he said. "You wouldn't hurt your own wife."

"Don't bet on it, Mr. Rhineheart. There's very little I wouldn't do to get my way in this matter. In that regard, Jessica's just one more obstacle."

When Rhineheart didn't respond, Kingston said, "Don't even think about trying to come near Jessica, Mr. Rhineheart. The house and the grounds are surrounded by security people. They have orders to shoot you on sight. As of now, Jessica's not being harmed. She's safe so long as you keep your mouth shut."

"I want to see her," Rhineheart said.

"That can be arranged," Kingston replied. "After the Derby, perhaps. We'll see."

"She comes to any harm," Rhineheart said, "and I'll kill you personally."

The threat didn't seem to faze Kingston, who said, "Warn off your colleagues, Mr. Rhineheart, and no harm will come to anyone, including Jessica."

"Don't worry," Rhineheart said. "I'll take care of that."

"You really care for Jessica, don't you? That's very touching, Mr. Rhineheart. I'll give her your best." The line went dead.

Over on the couch, Farnsworth had raised up and was looking at him. "I overheard your end of that."

"So did I," said McGraw from the bedroom doorway. She was wearing Rhineheart's bathrobe. It hung in folds on her, and trailed across the floor when she walked through the front room into the kitchen. She was carrying her cigarettes and lighter in her little fist. "I better make some coffee," she said.

Farnsworth and Rhineheart followed her into the kitchen. They sat down at the table while McGraw put on the coffeepot. She set cups and spoons and napkins in front of them, sat down, and they all lighted cigarettes.

Farnsworth said, "He threaten to kill his wife if we went to the police?"

Rhineheart nodded.

"You think he's bluffing?"

"I don't know," Rhineheart said. "He might be, but I can't take that chance."

Farnsworth shrugged. "No, I guess you can't."

"I don't think he's bluffing," McGraw said. "I think he's a fanatic. I think he'd do anything to win the Derby."

"Fact is," Farnsworth said, "if we went to the cops without any evidence they'd laugh at us anyway."

"You may be right," Rhineheart said.

"So what's going to happen?" McGraw said.

Rhineheart shrugged. "The bad guys are going to get away with it," he said angrily. "Make twelve million bucks and live happily ever after. How the fuck do I know what's going to happen?"

"Don't snap at me," McGraw shot back.

"I'm sorry," Rhineheart said.

"Case like this'll get on everybody's nerves," Farnsworth said.

McGraw said, "Maybe you'll think of something,

Rhineheart. Some last-minute solution. Something brilliant. You'll save her and get the bad guys and oh shit—" She burst into tears.

"Hey," Rhineheart said, patting her hand. "Take it easy, babe."

Farnsworth stood up. "I'll pour the coffee."

McGraw grabbed up a napkin and blew her nose. "Look at me. What's the matter with me?" She sniffled. "Private eyes aren't supposed to cry, are they?"

"Not in public anyway," Rhineheart said.

THIRTY

The three of them were still sitting there the next morning when the sun came up. Everyone got up and stretched. Rhineheart pulled up the blinds and took a peek at the world outside. It was Friday, the day before the Derby, and it was dawning bright and sunny.

He put on another pot of coffee, made a pan of scrambled eggs, and they ate breakfast. While McGraw got dressed, Rhineheart drove Farnsworth down to his office. He told the old man to go home and get some sleep. Farnsworth said he thought he might just drive over to the airport and check out Corrati's departure. Just for curiosity's sake. Rhineheart told him to be careful and to stay out of Corrati's way.

He drove back to the apartment and took McGraw home, telling her to take the day off and get some rest. She nodded and said she'd call him later.

He drove down to the office. The first thing he did was phone his service. Kate Sullivan had been trying to get hold of him. She had called last night and again this morning. What the hell was he going to say to her? He was probably going to have to tell her the truth.

He dialed her number, and as soon as she came on the line he could tell by her voice something was wrong.

"Michael?"

"Yeah."

"I've been trying to get in touch with you since yesterday afternoon."

"What's the problem?"

"I'm afraid I have some bad news."

"Let me guess," Rhineheart said. "The station doesn't want you covering the Walsh story any longer."

There was a short pause, then: "How did you know?"

"I been in the business awhile. It's the kind of shit that happens when you mess around with rich and powerful people. They put pressure on someone to stop you."

"Michael, listen, let me assure you, it's not simply a question of pressure. Since Carl Walsh's death was ruled an accident, my news director doesn't feel that the expense of an outside investigation is warranted. That's the way he put it."

"I see."

"I'm sorry, Michael."

"Don't worry about it," Rhineheart said.

"And, Michael," she said, "there'll be a check in the mail covering your fees through today."

"Don't you even want to know what I found out?" Rhineheart asked her.

"Michael . . . I'm sorry, but my career is at stake here."

"What about Carl Walsh?" Rhineheart said.

She didn't say anything.

Rhineheart raised his voice. "What about the story that was going to blow the town wide open?" The reason he was getting so angry, Rhineheart knew, was because he was backing off the case himself.

Kate Sullivan still didn't say anything.

"What about the simple fucking truth?"

She hung up the phone. Softly.

So much for Broadcast Journalism. On the local level. It was on a par, Rhineheart felt, with local detecting.

He spent the rest of the morning trying to call Jessica Kingston at the private number she had given him on Wednesday night.

But no one answered.

The mailman, a fat guy with white hair, arrived just before noon. He walked in and dropped a stack of letters on Rhineheart's desk.

"How ya doing?" he said.

"Not too good."

"How's the private detective business?"

"Not too great," Rhineheart said.

"Who's going to win the Derby?" the mailman asked.

"I don't know."

"The California horse," he said.

"Is that right?"

"He's a lock. I been following this horse since he was a two-year-old."

"I'm kind of busy," Rhineheart said.

"You're not very friendly," the mailman said.

"Get the fuck out of here," Rhineheart said. "Go waste someone else's time."

"You know what your trouble is?"

Rhineheart stood up.

"Okay, okay," the mailman said. "I'm leaving." He hustled out the door.

Rhineheart sat back down and began to sort absently through the mail. There was a bill from Southern Bell; a letter from Friendly Finance urging him to come in and meet with their team of professional loan consultants who could show him how to take advantage of their new low monthly interest rates; and a notice from the local federal bankruptcy court that a former client of Rhineheart's had listed him as one of the client's substantial creditors. There was an offer from two book clubs, and a record club, and a magazine publisher. And there was a lumpy 8 by 10 manila envelope with Rhineheart's name and office address scrawled across the front in wide, looping letters that looked familiar: the same handwriting he had seen on the photograph of Walsh and his wife. There was no return address on the envelope. Inside, was a cassette recording tape. The one Taggert had been looking for. A Sony, in a clear plastic case. Rhonda had said she might send him something that belonged to Carl.

Rhineheart opened the bottom drawer of his desk, and rummaged around and found the recorder, an old Panasonic. He plugged it in, put in the tape, and hit PLAY. The tape had a hollow, scratchy sound to it, but the voices were identifiable and understandable. The first voice he heard was Duke Kingston's resonant drawl.

KINGSTON: What is it you want, Walsh?

WALSH: I want to talk to you . . . about Royal Dancer.
(*A pause*)

KINGSTON: What about Royal Dancer?

WALSH: I know what's going on, Kingston.

KINGSTON: What are you talking about?

WALSH: I know what's going on with Dancer.

KINGSTON: What do you mean?

WALSH: Don't play no fucking word games with me,
Kingston. I'm telling you I know what's going on. I seen
you. I seen Doc Gilmore give the horse his last injection. I know about Lancelot. I know the whole fucking
thing. You and Gilmore and the redheaded dude. His
name is Lewis. You got some kind of drug nobody can
detect.

KINGSTON: Lower your voice. Someone might hear you.
(*A long pause*) What do you want?

WALSH: I want in. I want a cut. I want some fucking
money, Kingston.

KINGSTON: I don't see any problem with that.

WALSH: Good. You saw any problem, I'd have to think
about going to see the stewards. Or the state racing
commission. Or the cops.

KINGSTON: That would be a mistake.

WALSH: You think so?

KINGSTON: We'll work something out, Walsh. Of course,
I'll have to consult with my associates.

WALSH: Why don't you do that. And get back to me.
Soon.

KINGSTON: You have a number where I can reach you?

WALSH: I'll call you.

KINGSTON: Fine. I'll set up a meeting.

WALSH: Don't fuck me around, Kingston. You fuck me
around I'm going to see the Man.

KINGSTON: Don't get upset, Walsh. There's no need to
make threats. You'll be taken care of.

WALSH: I better be.

KINGSTON: Who knows about this, besides you, that is?

WALSH: None of your fucking business who knows about
it.

KINGSTON: You been going around shooting your mouth off about it, haven't you.

WALSH: What do you think—I'm a fucking dummy? Why would I tell anybody else?

KINGSTON: What about your buddy, the Mexican kid?

WALSH: Sanchez? Naw, he don't know nothing. Look, I got to get back to the barn now. I'll talk to you later.

The recording trailed off into silence. Rhineheart switched off the recorder. He stood up and walked over to the window. Below, on Main, a wino with a white beard stumbled into a bar across the street. A good-looking woman with long blonde hair came out of a building. She carried a briefcase and stepped briskly along the sidewalk. She had Rhineheart's vote for Businesswoman of the Year.

The tape was evidence. He could take it to Katz, or to the Commonwealth's Attorney, or to the Thoroughbred Protective Agency. It would be enough evidence to stop the Derby fix. And maybe even enough to put Kingston and Corrati in jail for a while. But he knew while he was listening to it that that wasn't what he was going to do with it.

He was going to trade the tape for Jessica Kingston's life.

Farnsworth wouldn't approve, Rhineheart knew. He would say play by the rules. The rules are all you got. Farnsworth had a code. Well, Rhineheart had something, too. He didn't know if it was a code, but it said that some things were more important than rules. Jessica Kingston was a lot more important than some code.

He dialed Cresthill Farms. The maid answered the phone. She said, "Mr. Kingston isn't taking any calls right now."

Rhineheart said, "You tell him that Rhineheart's calling about Royal Dancer and that if he doesn't get his ass on the phone in one minute he won't have one."

Thirty seconds later Kingston came on the line. His voice was tight with anger.

"I thought you had better sense than this, Mr. Rhineheart. I warned you what might happen if you continued to bother me."

"Listen to this." Rhineheart played the tape for Kingston.

"That's interesting material you have there," Kingston said, "but I don't see that it alters the situation any. You make a move to distribute that tape, and it's good-bye Jessica."

"I got a deal for you, Kingston."

"What kind of deal?"

"Simple. I give you the tape. You let Jessica go."

After a moment, Kingston said, "How do I know I can trust you?"

"I got the same problem, Kingston. We each want something badly. I guess we can trust that."

Kingston said, "You made yourself a deal, Mr. Rhineheart."

"We'll have to meet someplace," Rhineheart said. "Make the exchange. A public place."

"No problem," Kingston said. "There's a special thoroughbred auction at Keeneland tonight. In the sales pavilion. I'll arrange a seat for you."

Rhineheart thought it over. "All right," he said.

"Bring the tape," Kingston said, "and I'll bring Jessica."

THIRTY-ONE

According to the catalog, the two-year-old in the pavilion sales ring was a son of Raja Baba out of a Neartic mare. He was a lean and spindly-legged dark bay who stood calmly in the center of the ring. The electronic boards on either side of the podium identified the colt as HIP No. 214 and flashed the figure $2,500,000 to the audience—three hundred and fifty people seated in a semicircle in a glassed-in amphitheater.

From where Rhineheart sat—an aisle seat on a side row—the colt didn't look like he was worth any two million five. On the other hand what the hell did he know. Or care, for that matter. If the audience, a black-tie crowd of the rich and the super rich—Arab sheikhs, American potentates, and British royalty—was willing to bid the horse that high, that was cool with Rhineheart. After all, it was their money.

He was getting nervous. It was growing late, and the two seats to his right were still empty. There was no sign of Kingston. No sign of Jessica.

He got up and walked to the back of the room and went out into the hallway that circled the amphitheater. He lit a cigarette and looked around. The hallway was crowded. People pressed up against the glass to see inside the amphitheater. There were loudspeakers in the hallway so that everyone could hear the bidding. The Raja Baba colt was now up to three million.

He walked down the hallway. There were rooms with

banks of phones marked for long distance and international lines. Most of the phones were in use. The babble of accents and languages made the place sound like a foreign bazaar. He went into the restroom and washed his hands and looked at himself in the mirror. He sure wasn't much to look at. He left the restroom and walked back up the hallway. At the other end of the pavilion there was a bar and a glassed-in patio with some tables and chairs.

The Kingstons were seated at one of the tables.

They were alone. None of Kingston's men were around.

Rhineheart walked over to the table. Kingston looked nervous. Jessica had a grave look on her face. There was an empty drink in front of her.

He sat down across from her.

Kingston said, "You bring the tape?"

"Are you all right?" Rhineheart asked Jessica.

She nodded.

He took the tape out of his pocket and set it on the table.

Kingston reached across the table. His fingers closed around the plastic case.

Borchek and the big bearded guy walked into the patio. They stood near the door, watching the table.

Rhineheart said to Jessica, "It's a tape recording of your husband talking to Carl Walsh. It's evidence, but I had to give it to him. He threatened to kill you."

She nodded. "I understand, Michael."

"You can leave him now," Rhineheart said. "He won't hurt you. I'll make sure of that. Come back to Louisville with me. I'll take you wherever you want."

She shook her head. "I don't think I can do that."

"You don't understand," he said. "He threatened to kill you. I gave him the tape so he'd let you go."

"Yes," she said, "I know. I understand, but things are more complicated than that."

Kingston said, "He'll take you wherever you want to go, Jessica."

"Be quiet, Duke."

Kingston stood up. "Why don't you tell him the truth, Jessica?"

"Duke—"

He put his hand on her shoulder. "Tell him who you belong to."

She looked up at him. "You bastard." Her voice was icy.

Kingston looked over at Rhineheart. "You were one night in her life, mistah. Just like all the others. And you played the dupe. Right to the end. Without you, we never would've found the tape." He turned to his wife. "You ready?"

She spoke to Rhineheart. "I'm sorry, Michael."

"Sure."

She stood up. "I never wanted to hurt you."

"No," he said. "Of course not."

"Come on, Jessica," Kingston said, "you owe him a good-bye, but let's not drag the farewells out."

Rhineheart stood up and turned toward Kingston.

Borchek reached inside his coat.

Jessica stepped between her husband and Rhineheart.

"Good-bye, Michael."

She took Kingston's arm and together they walked out. Rhineheart stood there and watched them leave. Borchek and the bearded guy followed them.

Rhineheart sat back down. Kingston's words came back to him—like blows to the face. You were one night in her life. Just like all the others. You played the dupe. Right to the end.

He got up from the table and walked slowly over to the bar. A white-jacketed bartender slapped a fresh napkin down in front of him.

"What'll you have, sir?"

"You got bourbon?"

"Yes, sir."

"That's what I'll have."

"Straight up? On the rocks?"

"Yeah," he said. "That's right."

"Which one, sir?"

"Bring me the fucking bottle," Rhineheart said.

"Yes, sir."

"And a glass."

"Yes, sir."

* * *

Rhineheart wasn't sure how long he stayed there in the pavilion bar. He didn't remember the drive back to Louisville. He forgot how many bars he hit or how many drinks he had. All he knew was that one time when he looked up from a drink, McGraw was sitting next to him. They were in a honky-tonk bar on Market Street.

"What's a person like you doing in a place like this?" Rhineheart asked.

"Hunting for you, Rhineheart."

"Did you find me?"

"I guess so."

"How am I?"

"That's what I want to know."

"I'm fine," Rhineheart said. "I'm dying, but otherwise I'm fine."

"You're dying?"

"Maybe it just feels like it."

"How many drinks did you have?"

Rhineheart thought that over. "Seventy-three."

"You're drunk."

"I am?"

"Uh-huh. You're drunker than shit. And your knuckles are bleeding. And you got a big cut over your eye."

"How come?"

"Waitress says you been in three fights since you been here. Says you threw one guy through a plate glass window. Says you keep talking about some woman who messed you up."

"Yeah? Well, that sounds like a crock of shit. That doesn't sound like the Rhineheart I know. That sounds like some dumb-ass country song to me."

"What happened anyway?"

"Walsh's wife sent me a tape. It had Kingston's voice on it. Talking to Walsh. It was evidence. I traded it to Kingston for his wife, only it was all bullshit. She was in on the thing the whole time."

"Oh shit," McGraw said. "God damn!"

"That's what I say."

"You poor son of a bitch. You must be hurting."

"I'm dying."

"You're not dying. You're hurting and you're drunk, but you're not dying."

"It feels like I am." Rhineheart squinted past McGraw's shoulder. "Who's that ugly son of a bitch sitting next to you?"

"It's Farns," McGraw said.

Farnsworth nodded and said, "You don't look too good, kid."

"I'm sorry, old man."

"It's okay, kid."

"Naw, it's not okay. Don't fucking tell me it's okay. I know better. I blew it. I blew it bad. I broke the rules, old man. I fucked it up, and there ain't no getting around that."

"Everyone fucks up once in a while, kid."

"Yeah, but not like this, old man. I had the evidence in my hand, and I give it to him."

"You didn't make any copies?"

Rhineheart shook his head.

"That wasn't too good a move," Farnsworth said.

"That's what I'm telling you," Rhineheart said. "It was a bad move. I didn't make any good moves on this one."

"So what are you going to do about it?" Farnsworth said. "Sit around here and piss and moan and cry about it all night?"

Rhineheart nodded. "Yeah, that's what I'm thinking about doing."

"Well, forget it," McGraw said. "You're going home to bed, Rhineheart."

"Who says?"

"We do." McGraw got off the stool and came around and put her hand under Rhineheart's elbow. "Get his other arm," she told Farnsworth.

"You betcha, girlie."

THIRTY-TWO

When Rhineheart woke up the next morning he was lying fully clothed on his bed. His mouth tasted like a sewer and his head felt as if it were swollen twice its normal size. He felt more dead than alive. Otherwise, he seemed to be all right.

He got up slowly and carefully, undressed, and put on his sweat clothes and running shoes. He went outside. It was a beautiful Saturday morning in May. Derby Day. He got into the Maverick and started it up and drove over to the cinder track at Bellarmine.

He ran for two hours. He didn't count the laps or the miles. He just kept running until he felt he had sweated all the booze and all the poison out of his body. When he was through he drove back home and took a long shower, shaved, and got dressed. A tweed sport coat. Gray slacks. Black, soft leather loafers. He put on his watch: it was 12:05.

Out at the Downs they had opened the gates four hours ago. By now the infield was half full. The first race had already been run. On Derby Day they moved post time for the first race to 11:30 and set the races an hour apart. The Derby, the eighth race on the card, was scheduled to go off at 5:30.

He went out to the Maverick and drove over to a Convenient store on Bardstown Road. He bought the Derby edition of the *Daily Racing Form* and a Derby program and a plant, a leafy green treelike plant that was set in a pot.

On the way downtown he switched on the radio to the station that featured all-day coverage of the Derby. The reporter was interviewing a celebrity who was attending his first Derby. The celebrity was telling the reporter how nice it was to be able to get out and meet his many fans.

Downtown, there were roadblocks at some of the main intersections. Most of the stores were closed and the downtown streets were empty of people. Everyone in town was either out at the track or at home having a Derby party.

He parked in a no-parking zone in front of police headquarters and took an elevator to the third floor. Katz was sitting behind his desk, typing up another report. He didn't seem particularly glad to see Rhineheart.

Rhineheart sat down in a chair next to the desk and told Katz the whole story from beginning to end.

Katz sat there patiently and listened to everything Rhineheart had to say. When Rhineheart was finished Katz stood up and began pacing back and forth. He said, "Jesus, that's some tale you got there, peeper. Three murders. One of the most prominent families in Kentucky. A plot to fix the biggest horse race in the world, no less. Big-time gamblers. Wonder drugs that can't be traced. There's just one problem."

"What's that, Katz?"

"Evidence," Katz said. "You got no evidence. You saw this. You overheard that. I got your word this other thing happened. Somebody shot at you. You didn't report it to the police. Someone else offered you a bribe. Only, it was in the form of a job offer, which as far as I know, Rhineheart, hasn't been ruled illegal by any court I know anything about. You show me a syringe you could have found somewhere. You got an airport locker key you say you found in a motel room of a dead guy whose body you didn't report—which is a fucking felony, by the way, not to mention you B and E'd the room." Katz stopped pacing. "You tell me a story about some tape you say you don't have no more. I take your story to my superior officer, you know what happens? They give me an early release from the department. Mental disability."

Rhineheart got to his feet.

"I'm sorry, peeper," Katz said. "I'd like to help you out.

You're a stand-up dude. You got balls. But I'm not crazy. I don't go out of my way to fuck with people who got as much power as Duke Kingston and Calvin Clark. You better not, either."

On his way out the door, Rhineheart said, "I'll see you around, Katz."

Farnsworth was asleep. His eyes were shut tight and he was snoring away, but when Rhineheart sat down in the hard chair across from his desk, the old man's eyelids snapped open and he blinked a couple of times and said, "Kid, how's it going?"

"I bought a plant today," Rhineheart said.

Farnsworth gave him a funny look.

"McGraw thought the office needed some color."

Farnsworth shrugged. "Well, maybe it does. Maybe it does. Hell, maybe *this* place could use some plants." He looked around. "Nahh. This place is beyond help."

Rhineheart told Farnsworth about his visit to Katz. The old man shook his head and said, "I didn't expect no different. Katz ain't a bad guy, but he can't stand up to people like Kingston."

Rhineheart took an envelope out of his pocket and handed it to Farnsworth. "There's a check in there. I think it covers everything. You let me know if it doesn't."

"Sure." Farnsworth stuck the envelope in his pocket without looking at it. "You want to talk about the case, kid?"

"I don't think so," Rhineheart said.

"There ain't much to say, is there?"

"Except that it's over. And we lost."

The old man nodded. "I been losing all my life, it seems like. Betting the slow horse, getting the bad card, taking the wrong case. In some ways *all* the cases are wrong cases. Being a private eye, kid, is a way of losing. So is life. The longer you stick around the more things you lose. And it doesn't get any easier. This one was a loser right from the beginning. The fix was in. Only we never seen it." The old man sighed. "I talk too goddamn much." He looked at Rhineheart. "So what are you going to do this afternoon?"

"I thought I might stop by the office," Rhineheart said. "Check the mail. See who called."

"You want some company?"

"Not today," Rhineheart said. He stood up and walked to the door. "Old man, I'll see you around."

"Kid," Farnsworth said, "it was a pleasure working with you again. Gimme a call sometime."

At the office McGraw was sitting behind her typewriter waiting for him.

"Isn't this your off day?"

"I just stopped by for a few minutes," she said. "How do you feel?"

"Like shit," he said. He squinted at her. "You and Farnsworth take me home last night?"

McGraw nodded. "And poured you into bed."

"I appreciate it, babe." Rhineheart set the plant down on his desk.

"What's with the plant?"

"You were right the other day," he said. "Place needs a little brightening up."

"That's a Weeping Fig," McGraw said. "*Ficus benjamina*." She came over and picked up the plant and took it back over to her desk. "They like sunlight," she said. "And a little water."

"I went to see Katz," Rhineheart said.

"How'd that go?"

"Not too well." He walked over and looked out the window. Outside were the same old streets.

"Is it over, Rhineheart?"

Rhineheart nodded. "It looks like it, yeah."

"They're going to get away with it, aren't they?"

"Probably."

"You want to talk about it?"

"Not really."

"Want me to hang around for a while?"

Rhineheart shook his head. "I'll be all right, babe."

McGraw picked up her purse and walked to the door. She stopped. "Guess what?"

"Huh?"

"Vogue has a good movie this evening."

"What's playing?"

"Grapes of Wrath."

Grapes of Wrath. Henry Fonda. Jane Darwell. John Carradine. The little Swedish guy. What was his name? Directed by John Ford. Written by John Steinbeck. Photographed by Gregg Toland, the same guy who shot *Kane.* "What time?" Rhineheart asked.

"Seven-thirty. Plus, popcorn's twenty cents to the first fifty customers."

"Sounds too good to pass up."

"Meet you out front."

"I'll try to make it, babe."

She walked out the door. Rhineheart went over and sat down at his desk. The mail had been delivered. There were some letters and a large envelope from Reardon at Midtown Investigations. It was information on Lewis and Thoroughbred Security. Rhineheart didn't bother opening it. He put his feet up and lit a cigarette.

After a while he turned on the radio, an FM station that featured jazz and blues. For a couple of hours, Rhineheart sat and smoked and listened to the music.

Late in the afternoon the phone started to ring. Rhineheart reached for it, then stopped. He didn't know who was calling, and the thing was, he really didn't want to know. He didn't want to get involved in anyone else's life. He was burned out. It was time to pull back, retrench. Hide. When the phone wouldn't stop ringing, he got up and walked out of the office. He got in the Maverick, started the car, and took off. He was halfway out to the Downs before he realized where he was going.

THIRTY-THREE

Rhineheart took Third Street south as far as he could—until he came up against roadblocks. A young kid in a blue Adidas T-shirt charged him ten bucks to park on someone's front lawn. He walked the rest of the way, a couple of blocks down Third to Central and along Central past the souvenir peddlers and the T-shirt booths and balloon hawkers to the Downs. There were people wandering around in front of the clubhouse and grandstand entrances, and cops everywhere.

Near the cabstand he bought a clubhouse ticket from a scalper for a hundred dollars. The scalper, a fat, bald-headed guy, had a pair of binoculars hanging from a string around his thick neck. Rhineheart offered him twenty dollars for the binoculars. He whipped them off and held out his hand for the twenty.

Rhineheart walked through the parking lot to the Longfield Avenue entrance. He looked at his watch as he went through the gate: 4:50. The Derby would go to post in forty minutes.

He made his way through the crowded clubhouse grounds, skirting throngs of stylishly dressed people. Every other woman seemed to be wearing a fashionable hat, and everyone's clothes were bright and summery. Large groups of people surrounded the garden areas where TV cameras had been set up and celebrities were being interviewed. All the benches in the clubhouse garden were occupied.

The paddock was encircled by a mass of people straining to get a look at the Derby horses being led around the enclosure by their handlers. On a scaffold above the paddock, a TV camera crew recorded the scene. The huge tote board blinked and flashed the odds and amounts of money bet in WIN, PLACE, and SHOW columns.

Rhineheart pushed through the crowd up to the fence and saw Duke Kingston standing in the cleared area in the center of the paddock where the owners and their entourage gathered before the race. Kingston was dressed in a blue blazer and light-colored slacks and was wearing a regimental tie. He had a drink in his hand and was chatting volubly with a group of well-dressed, important-looking people that included, among others, the governor of the Commonwealth.

Jessica Kingston was not there.

Borchek was standing near Kingston. Clark was in the crowd, and so was Hughes, but Rhineheart couldn't see Gilmore or Lewis.

A little farther along the paddock, Howard Taggert stood chatting with a smaller group of people.

Rhineheart noticed Royal Dancer among the horses that were being led around. The colt's ears were pricked and his head was up. He looked alert, maybe a little skittish. He didn't look as if he had been drugged, but Rhineheart was no expert on the subject.

The jockeys appeared at the far end of the paddock, and the handlers led their horses into the individual stalls where the trainers began to saddle them.

A network reporter with a mike in his hand and a cameraman with a minicam on his shoulder walked from stall to stall conducting last-minute interviews.

Gilmore entered the paddock, walked over to Kingston, and whispered something in his ear. Kingston smiled and nodded.

In a few moments, Rhineheart knew, the paddock judge would walk to the front of the paddock area and call out, "Riders up." The trainers would help the jocks onto their mounts and the grooms or handlers would take hold of the bridles and lead the horses along the paddock runway toward the tunnel. The call to the post would begin to sound over the loudspeaker system.

Rhineheart had seen enough. He decided that what he needed was a drink. Turning, he walked up the stairs to the terrace and through the doors to the main clubhouse bar. It was crowded. The tables were all full and customers were three deep at the bar, but the bartender, a thick-necked ex-cop named Skip, recognized Rhineheart, and made a little space for him at the end of the bar.

"What'll you have, Rhineheart?"

"Double bourbon. On the rocks."

"You got it."

He set the drink down in front of Rhineheart, who started to reach for it and hesitated, the same kind of half-ass move he'd made a week before when the phone on his desk started to ring. Rhineheart picked up the glass, then set it back down, untouched.

"I get your drink wrong?" Skip asked.

Rhineheart shook his head. "*I* did."

He squinted up at the TV above the bar. The horses were leaving the paddock. The call to the post was being played. You could hear it, Rhineheart knew, all over the racetrack. Even against the noise of the bar, the notes sounded sharp and distinct.

On TV the scene shifted from the paddock to the track where the horses began to appear, emerging from the tunnel. They were picked up by outriders on stable ponies and led down the track toward the finish line.

Rhineheart put a ten on the bar and told Skip he'd catch him another time. He left the bar and walked down the hallway, stepping outside just as the band in the infield struck up "My Old Kentucky Home."

The clubhouse crowd rose as one and began to sing. Across the way, the infield was a solid sea of people, all standing and singing. Below, on the track, the horses circled around and began to parade back up the track.

Rhineheart climbed the steps to the top row of the clubhouse and found his seat. It was high up in Section G, under the overhang. The Kingstons' private box was below to his right. Fifty, maybe seventy-five yards away.

Over on the backstretch the horses began to warm up.

Rhineheart looked around—at the crowd in the stands and in the infield—and wondered what the hell he was doing there. Had he come out here to see how it all ended? To see if the fix worked? Maybe he was there just to get another look at Jessica Kingston.

He raised the binoculars to his eyes and focused them and caught his breath when he saw her as clear as if she were seated next to him. No matter what she had done, she would always have that kind of effect on him. She was wearing a rose-colored dress and dark glasses and a wide-brimmed hat that was pulled down low over one side of her face. There was a radiance about her today, Rhineheart saw. She looked more beautiful than ever. She was the kind of woman, he thought, for whom you did whatever it took —amassed a fortune, fixed a Derby, traded some evidence.

He shifted the glasses slightly to the right and Duke Kingston's face leaped into view. Kingston looked half-juiced. His eyes were liquidy and a loose grin flashed on and off his face. He was saying something to Jessica, but she didn't appear to be listening to him. Rhineheart panned around the box—Gilmore, Clark, Hughes, Lewis, and Borchek. Except for Corrati, all the principals. He felt a curious detachment, as if these people and what was about to happen were something that didn't really concern him.

He lowered the binoculars. The horses had finished warming up and were moving toward the starting gate. He looked down at the infield tote board. TIME OF DAY: 5:35. MINUTES TO POST: 1.

He glanced over at the odds. Blustering was the favorite at 2 to 1. Taggert's horse, Calabrate, was 7 to 2. Royal Dancer had come down slightly in the betting and was now 6 to 1. He would pay $14.00 to win—200,000 times $14.00 was what? Almost $3,000,000, Rhineheart calculated.

He looked back up the track and saw that the horses had arrived at the starting gate and were beginning to load in.

The track announcer's voice came booming out over the loudspeaker: "The horses have reached the starting gate. It is now post time. And . . . they're at the post."

The crowd instantly quieted, then let out a great roar

when the doors clanged open and the horses burst from the gate.

Royal Dancer broke alertly from the number 3 post and sprinted quickly to the front. Montez, hunched up over Dancer, his knees high in the stirrups, the reins gathered loosely in his hands, steered him over to the rail.

On the outside, Calabrate rushed up to take second. The dark gray horse, Blustering, lay third on the inside as the field of horses swept down the stretch.

Royal Dancer had a one-length lead when he passed the sixteenth pole. To Rhineheart the colt seemed to be running easily. His stride looked smooth and powerful as he raced past the finish line for the first time and entered the clubhouse turn.

Rhineheart put the glasses on the Kingstons' box. They were all on their feet, cheering.

He panned over to the race and caught Royal Dancer in a burst of speed in the middle of the turn. Royal Dancer's stride lengthened and he began to pull away from Calabrate and the rest of the field. By the time he rounded the turn and hit the backstretch Dancer had drawn out to a three-length lead.

Unchallenged, he sailed down the backstretch, gradually increasing his lead.

Rhineheart looked over at the board. The fractions the colt was setting were blistering—.22 for the quarter, .45 for the half, six furlongs in 1.09.3. They seemed much too fast for a mile-and-a-quarter race.

Royal Dancer moved into the far turn with a big lead. Four, maybe four and a half lengths. From across the track it looked as if Blustering had taken over second. In the middle of the turn Royal Dancer disappeared from view. Rhineheart could see Montez's royal blue and green silks bobbing up and down above the line of the crowd.

A few seconds later Royal Dancer came out of the turn and hit the top of the stretch. He was running a little wide but his stride was easy and fluid.

The crowd in the stands was on its feet, roaring, anticipating a big upset. Royal Dancer swung out to the center of the track and Montez hit him once right-handed and set him down for the drive. The colt drew off. The drug seemed to be doing its work. As Royal Dancer passed the eighth pole his lead was six lengths. They're not going to catch him, Rhineheart thought. No way.

A few strides later, it happened.

Without any warning, Royal Dancer's head dropped down suddenly and the jock, Montez, went flying, pitching forward onto the track. Montez rolled under the rail, and Royal Dancer's stride slowed abruptly, becoming a series of stiff, lurching motions. He continued on for six, eight, ten more lengths, but he was no longer racing. He was hobbling. He pulled up finally, his right foreleg stuck out at a crazy angle.

Royal Dancer had broken down.

The rest of the field, led by Blustering, came pounding down the stretch. They surged past and around the lame horse and headed for the finish line. But by then Rhineheart wasn't watching the race anymore. He had run down the stairs and was moving along the aisle toward Kingston's box, where a commotion of some kind had erupted.

The aisle was thick with people. Rhineheart had to push his way through. He was too far away to see clearly, but it looked as if Kingston was struggling with someone in the box. Through a break in the crowd, Rhineheart saw that Kingston had his hands around Gilmore's neck and was choking him. Gilmore broke free and pushed Kingston away. Kingston had a wild look about him, as if he had gone crazy. The chairs in the box were overturned. Jessica stood to one side, a look of shock and disbelief on her face.

Only a small group of people, those in the immediate area, were aware of the disturbance in Kingston's box. Everyone else was watching the finish of the Derby. The roar of the crowd was deafening.

Rhineheart was still fifteen feet away when he saw Kingston look wildly around, then reach over and grab Borchek's gun out of its hip holster. He aimed it at Gilmore whose back was turned to him and fired. The shot was muffled. It sounded like the snap of a firecracker against the noise of the crowd. Gilmore fell to his knees. Someone screamed.

Kingston's head jerked around. He looked straight at Rhineheart, who was rushing up the aisle. He doesn't recognize me, Rhineheart thought. Then Kingston raised his weapon and aimed it at him.

Jessica Kingston turned toward Rhineheart. She started to raise her hand to him and stopped in mid-gesture. She said something Rhineheart couldn't hear, then turned and spoke to her husband. She stepped in front of the gun just as Kingston fired. Rhineheart saw her body recoil when the bullet slammed into her. She fell slowly to the ground.

Kingston watched her fall, a horrified look on his face. The gun was still in his hand, still pointed at Rhineheart. As he closed the last few feet of ground, Rhineheart heard a voice off to the right say, "Drop the weapon and freeze, mister," and he looked over and saw a Kentucky state trooper in a brown uniform standing in the aisle with his gun pointed at Kingston.

Kingston, dazed, turned toward the trooper with the weapon in his hand. The trooper shot Kingston twice in the chest, and Kingston fell over backward into the adjoining box.

Rhineheart dropped to one knee, and cradled Jessica Kingston's head in his arms. She was conscious, but just barely. She looked up at him, her face pale and scared.

"Michael."

"Yeah."

"Michael?"

"Yes."

"I'm sorry."

"It's all right, babe," Rhineheart said. "It doesn't matter."

She looked up at Rhineheart and started to smile, then winced and closed her eyes and died. Her body went heavy in his arms. He picked her up as if he were going to carry her somewhere. Then he saw a circle of faces watching him and he realized where he was and what had happened and he laid her down gently on the concrete floor. He knelt next to her body until they brought the stretcher.

THIRTY-FOUR

Jessica Kingston's funeral was held on the Tuesday following the Derby. It was a private ceremony. She was buried in her father's family plot in the Frankfort Cemetery, high on the side of a hill that overlooked the dome of the capitol and a bend in the Kentucky River.

It was raining. The weather had turned cold. The wind was sharp and bitter.

The minister read from the book of Common Prayer. *I am the resurrection and the life . . . He that believeth in me . . . yet shall he live: and whosoever liveth and believeth in me, shall never die . . .*

We come into this world with nothing, and it is certain we can carry nothing out.

Rhineheart stood there in the rain with his head bowed. He tried to recall something that Farnsworth had said about losing. But he couldn't bring it to mind. When the prayer was ended they lowered the casket into the grave and Rhineheart raised his head and walked down the hill and got into his car and drove back home to Louisville.

ADDENDUM

Blustering won the Derby. He paid $6.80 to win, $4.00 to place, and $2.80 to show. Taggert's horse, Calabrate was second. A long shot named Marking Ink was third.

The mile and a quarter was run in 2:01.2. The winner earned $450,000. Second place was worth $235,000.

Duke Kingston was pronounced dead at the scene. Harrison Gilmore was rushed to Methodist Hospital, where he underwent emergency surgery to repair a shattered spleen. He died on the operating table at 9:12 P.M. on Derby Day.

The sesamoid bone in Royal Dancer's right front leg had snapped under the pressure of the race. The colt was operated on that evening by a crack team of veterinary surgeons. The operation was not successful.

Three months after the race John Hughes was brought up on charges of attempting to fix a horse race before the Kentucky State Racing Commission. He was found guilty and banned for life from all thoroughbred tracks in North America.

The Louisville Police Department investigated the deaths of Felix Sanchez, Tammy Shea, and Carl Walsh. The evidence was presented to a grand jury, but no indictments were returned.

Six months after the Derby, Angelo Corrati was gunned down in the alley behind the Kitty Kat Club by person or persons unknown. The police are still investigating his murder.

Kathleen Sullivan left Channel Six and went to work for

a CBS affiliate in Nashville, where she is now an anchor-woman.

William Lewis, the chemist, was found guilty in federal court of deliberately falsifying his income tax returns. He is awaiting sentencing.

Calvin Clark continues to live and practice law in Frankfort, Kentucky. Just the other day he was appointed to the Governor's Commission on the Arts.

Rhineheart has moved. His new office is on Market, around the corner from the Hall of Justice. The rent is cheaper.

McGraw is up to twenty-five words a minute.